THE SHROUDED TOME

TEN FORGOTTEN FABLES

RONALD KELLY

D & T
PUBLISHING

For Erica Robyn Metcalf
Much thanks for your kindness & friendship,
and for loving my style of Southern storytelling.

ATTRIBUTIONS

Introduction © 2023 by Ronald Kelly

"*Strong Steps*" was published as an Elemental chapbook, Thunderstorm Books, 2016

"*Midnight Tide*" appeared in the ebook collection *Midnight Tide & Other Seaside Shivers*, Crossroad Press, 2016

"*The Dark Tribe*" appeared in *Tri-State Fantasist*, 1989

"*Tyrophex-14*" appeared in *The Earth Strikes Back*, edited by Richard Chizmar, 1994

"*The Boxcar*" appeared in *After Hours Magazine*, 1989

"*Dust Devils*" appeared in *2AM Magazine*, 1989

"*Better Than Breadcrumbs*" appeared in *Cemetery Dance Magazine*, 1989

"*Romicide*" appeared in *Cemetery Dance Magazine*, 1996

"*Thinning the Herd*" appeared in *2AM Magazine*, 1992

"*The General's Arm*" appeared in *Mia Moja*, Thunderstorm Books, 2014

CONTENTS

INTRODUCTION

All writers desire their work to be cherished and remembered. If they are fortunate enough, they will write a few novels and short stories that stand the test of time... tales that readers enjoy and talk about for years after they are committed to ink and paper. These are the kind of tomes that earn an honored spot on bookshelves in homes and public libraries, and, if the planets align favorably, even on the racks of brick and mortar bookstores.

But, many times, novels, novellas, and short stories are written, published, read, and then pass into oblivion. Forgotten, misplaced, unattainable. It is not necessarily because they are substandard compared to your other work; they may very well be better than some of your more popular tales. Sometimes it is how they are published and where they appear that limits their accessibility. They could be presented in limited editions to be published and collected, but are not readily available to the general reading public. Some-times, they are featured in obscure periodicals or magazines from the distant past. Sometimes you write and love them, but they never find the home they truly deserve... and are never read by anyone other than the one who created them.

These are the ones that suffer the fate of the premature burial.

Shrouded and unceremoniously laid to rest. Stories that languish in shadow and darkness, abandoned and underappreciated.

Within these pages, you will find ten such tales of Southern horror that have not been available for quite a while; tales that many who enjoy my storytelling have missed over the years, due to one reason or another. Novellas, novelettes, and short stories that I wrote with great hope and anticipation, but then faded and became relics of the past... some fairly recently, while some haven't been in print since the small press days of the late 1980s and early 1990s.

In this volume, I have lifted the shroud to give you a peek underneath. Like the good Doctor Frankenstein, I have sewn them together and resurrected them into a palpable and – hopefully – enjoyable collection, to live and breathe again.

True, you may find traces of dust and cobwebs, even a touch of rigor mortis here and there. But, as lovers of dark and twisted prose, isn't that what we crave to explore and indulge in?

Many Happy Nightmares!

Ronald Kelly
    Brush Creek, Tennessee
    February 2023

STRONG STEPS

ED MYERS FOUND himself standing in the center of a crosswalk. Abandoned, alone, without benefit of the two things that gave him the stability he needed in life... at least physically so.

His crutches.

It was a frigid winter's evening, perhaps in January or early February.

In the dim light of dusk, traces of old snow could be seen in pale patches on the sidewalks and icicles hung jaggedly from the over-hangs of nearby shops. At first, the two-lane street on which he stood seemed dry and safe enough for pedestrian travel. But as he shifted his weight, he found his footing to be precarious at best. A thin layer of solid ice covered the pavement beneath his feet. The soles of his shoes slid upon the frosty coating, giving him no traction.

Ed struggled to maintain his balance, but his lack of proper muscle control made that action near to impossible. Without his crutches—which had practically been a physical part of him since the young age of two—Ed had difficulty navigating on solid ground, let alone on an unstable surface such as a solid sheet of black ice.

He caught his reflection in a storefront window on the opposite side of the street; a short, stocky fellow in his mid-forties with thinning brown hair with a trace of gray at the temples. He looked incredibly *wrong* minus his crutches... like a slouchy, life-sized rag doll on the verge of collapse, or at least that was how he appeared in *his* eyes.

Abruptly, he lost his footing and fell, landing hard on his back in the street. For a moment, that familiar feeling of embarrassment and incompetence threatened to overtake him, but he quickly quelled the emotions. He had never been one for feeling sorry for himself, and he certainly wasn't about to start now. Ed waited for his lost breath to return, then struggled to climb to his feet.

Again, the ice won out and he found himself floundering on his hands and knees. He looked around for assistance. People milled around on the sidewalks on both sides of the street, but seemed oblivious to his plight. Ed looked up and down the avenue and was relieved to see no cars coming in either direction. If one showed up all of a sudden, he would surely be run over.

Ed was again attempting to rise to his feet when he spotted a young boy of six standing on the curb to his left. His heart pounded as he realized that it was his own son, Daniel. The dark-haired boy simply stood there and stared at him, obviously upset and confused, as if at a loss at what to do next. He seemed torn between running for help and attempting to assist his father.

"Stay where you are, Daniel!" Ed called out to him, forcing a smile of reassurance. "Don't worry... I'll be okay." His cheerful words echoed in his mind like a lie, though. Unless he could make it out of the street and back to the safety of the sidewalk, he was utterly helpless.

Ed regained his footing for a moment and nearly stood erect. Then the ice took him again and he was back where he was before, bruised and humiliated. Ed looked over at his son and was shocked to find that he was no longer on the curb. Searching frantically, he spotted him several yards down the sidewalk, walking away, hand-in-hand with a complete stranger. Due to the evening gloom, he found it difficult to make out the abductor. All he knew was that the man was tall and lean, with dark hair pulled tightly into a ponytail at the back.

"Stop!" he screamed fearfully. "That's my son! Bring him back! Please, bring him back!"

Before his frantic cries could reach the pair, however, he heard the roaring of an engine behind him, slowly increasing in volume and intensity. Startled, Ed turned to see a large vehicle barreling toward him swiftly, the headlights growing larger and brighter with each approaching second.

And beyond the damning lights, rang laughter, deeply resonant and cruel, amused at his predicament and totally devoid of mercy or compassion.

The following morning, Ed called his brother in Iowa.

"I had the nightmare again... last night," he told him.

Randy Myers waited patiently for Ed to complete his statement. His brother suffered from a stuttering problem on account of his Cerebral Palsy. "The one about the crosswalk?" he asked.

"Yes... except that it was different this time. Daniel was there... on a street corner. While I was trying to get up, someone took him."

"Took him? You mean, abducted him?"

Ed sighed with frustration. "That's right. And I couldn't do anything to help him."

"It was only a dream, Eddie."

"Nightmare. There's a big difference."

"Yeah, I suppose so," allowed Randy. "And you saw the head-lights, too?"

Ed was silent for a moment. "That's another thing that was different. The one driving the car, truck... whatever... *laughed* at me." He shuddered at the distant echo of that sinister laughter. "It was hideous... like the Devil himself."

Randy couldn't help but chuckle. "There you go with your devils." Ed Myers was a devout horror fan; an avid reader of dark fiction and watcher of macabre cinema. As kids, he and his brother had possessed a fascination with William Peter Blatty's *The Exorcist*. Ed had read the book in junior high; the next best thing without actually being allowed to see the movie. Also, their father had once told them a supposedly true account of demon possession and exorcism performed in Iowa, not far from their hometown of Ames. Ed had always claimed that the film of *The Exorcist* was the ultimate movie of Good versus Evil.

"Well, it was so *real*," Ed told him. "Not like the other times."

For a while, they talked about family and how things were back in Ames. Ed had moved to Ocean Springs, Mississippi, on the Gulf Coast, when he had married in 2003. His wife was a mechanical engineer at the naval base in nearby Pascagoula. They had one child, Daniel Enrique Myers—a fun-loving six-year-old who was the light of his father's life.

Randy hated to ask the question, but knew that he should. "So, how are things going with you and Maribel?"

A long, painful pause. "They're not. But I keep hoping... praying... that things will change for the better. I love her and Daniel too much to believe otherwise."

"I know, Eddie," Randy replied. "I'm praying, too."

Ed and his wife were recently separated. Ed had always hungered for the stability of a family of his own; a loving wife and child to balance the scales between normalcy and being "special." Maribel had apparently underestimated the challenges and lifestyle changes necessary in a relationship with someone physically disabled and she was, at least for now, unable to cope with it. Ed still loved her, both still treated each other with kindness and respect, and both shielded Daniel from their strained relationship as best they could.

When their conversation was finally done, an awkward silence occupied the phone line. The two siblings both missed each other immensely and parting, even vocally, was difficult. "Well, take care of yourself, little brother," Randy told him. "And I wouldn't worry about that nightmare. You've handled tougher things than bad dreams before." His brother's lifelong struggle with Cerebral Palsy had blessed him with strengths that even Ed wasn't quick to acknowledge. He possessed a grace, dignity, and determination that others in his situation might normally lack.

Ed laughed. "No sweat. Besides, dreams can't hurt you, can they?"

Voicing that simple statement, Ed Myers was unaware of how very mistaken he truly was.

Edward Alan Myers was born in 1964, over three months premature. Due to complications of such an early birth, he suffered from Cerebral Palsy. The love and support of his family, and the assistance of the medical community, especially the Easter Seal Center in Des Moines, Iowa, had set him on a solid pathway to living and dealing with his handicap. Ed had much to overcome from the very beginning of his life, and every day thereafter, but his perseverance and positive outlook had made him an inspiration to those who knew and loved him, although Ed's humble attitude was such that he failed to acknowledge his strengths in the same way that those around him did.

Owing to his condition, Ed was limited in the types of physical activity he was able to perform. He was not wheelchair bound, but walked with the aid of crutches, which he had mastered early in life. Ed's coordination challenges and lack of smooth muscle control also made it impossible for him to drive. Still, he took the unique life that God had given him and made the most of it. He had earned a bachelor's degree in Journalism from Iowa State University, hoping to become a sports journalist. Although he had written columns and articles for his hometown paper, the *Ames Tribune*, Ed had, so far, been unable to find gainful employment in his chosen field, mostly because of his physical challenges. If anything threatened to crack through his hard shell of determination and strength, that one disappointment was it.

Until recently, Ed had lived a happy and contented life in Ocean Springs. Still, he was secure in his Catholic faith, which sustained him spiritually and gave him the strength to tackle anything the world—and his disabilities—challenged him with.

But, following his most recent nightmare of the icy crosswalk, Ed had no earthly idea that both he and his faith would be put to the test in the most severe ways imaginable.

The following night, Ed endured another nightmare... but not the recurring one that he had experienced most of his adult life.

He found himself on a sandy beach at the edge of the Gulf Coast. It was a familiar spot—West Ship Island—one he, Maribel, and Daniel had sometimes visited in the balmy months of summer. He found himself there only with Daniel, which was peculiar since he would have never made the trip by himself. Ed found it near to impossible to move about in heavy sand, be it with crutches or a wheelchair. Whenever he visited the beach—which was rarely—the experience turned out to be more frustrating than enjoyable.

Still, in this particular dreamscape, he was there without concern, sitting in a beach chair, while Daniel built a sand castle a few yards away. "Don't get too close to the water," he called to the boy. Daniel nodded and smiled, continuing to mold damp sand into a fortress fit for the bravest and most stalwart of knights.

Ed sat and read a hardcover of Stephen King's *Under the Dome,* while Daniel played. A warm ocean breeze blew inland, ruffling his hair, making him drowsy. Soon the lines of the book began to blur and grow hard to follow, and, without warning, he drifted to sleep.

He awoke to find the sun several hours lower in the vast blue sky. He looked at the castle and found it deserted. Not only that, but someone had maliciously stomped it into mounds of formless sand. Had Daniel done it? It wasn't his son's nature to be so destructive, especially to something he had taken so much time and pride constructing.

Suddenly, a feeling of dread filled him. Come to think of it... where was Daniel?

"He is there," stated a voice from behind him. "In the ocean."

Ed looked toward the sea and was shocked to see Daniel chest-deep in the churning water. The tide was coming in and wave after coursing wave hit the boy, the whitecaps striking him forcefully, driving him under the surface.

"Mother Mary!" Ed exclaimed, aware of his blasphemy. He reached for his crutches, intending to rise and go to his son. But they were nowhere to be found.

"Looking for these?" Again that voice; deep, like the echo from a cavern, and edged with a distinctive hint of meanness.

Ed rose to his knees and turned his head. Behind him stood a tall man, tanned and leanly muscled, dressed only in faded blue jeans and scuffed cowboy boots. His clean-shaven face was strong and handsome, and his black hair—pulled back into a ponytail that hung between his shoulder blades—was such a hue of ebony that it nearly had a blue sheen to it, much like Superman in the comic book. Along the stranger's right arm, from elbow to the tips of his fingers, was an elaborate and disturbing tattoo that made the appendage resemble a dark green viper. Shiny black eyes were etched upon the knobs of his knuckles; eyes that almost seemed to roll and blink of their own accord, although Ed knew that it must be a trick his mind was playing on him.

In the man's hands were Ed's crutches... held only inches away.

"Please... give them to me," stammered Ed, reaching out. "I... I must go... to him."

The man seemed to take great delight in keeping the crutches from Ed's grasp. "Not so fast," he said. "What would you do if you had them? You would never make it across the beach fast enough to save him."

The man's voice was so silky smooth and steeled with authority and self confidence that it made Ed doubt the validity of his own intentions. He looked back and saw Daniel several yards further in the ocean, his head disappearing for a long moment, then breaking the surface once again, eyes frightened, mouth gasping for air. Ed knew that the six-year-old could not last for very much longer.

When Ed turned back toward the man, he found the crutches missing entirely. "My crutches! Please…where are they?"

"In the time you utter a single sentence, he could be lying at the bottom of the ocean," the tall man said contemptuously. "If you ask me, I will save him."

Something about the man with the snake tattoo conjured fear in Ed. But he submitted to his wishes for the sake of his child. "Okay. Please… please, go to him… quickly."

The man smiled at him with strong, white teeth that appeared almost wolfish in appearance. "Beg for it… or Daniel is lost."

Tears of panic had bloomed in Ed's eyes now. "Please… oh, please… save my son!"

The tattooed man laughed and, instantly, Ed realized who he was. He was the driver that had careened toward him on the street with the icy crosswalk. The haunting voice, full of cruel mirth and darkness, concealed behind the blazing headlights of his nightmare.

"Pathetic fool!" the man snapped, and then walked past Ed's kneeling form. He moved almost leisurely, as though time had no bearing on the situation at all. Ed prayed to God and the saints as the dark man waded into the advancing surf. The churning waters first covered his boots, and then rose to his knees and, eventually, the waistband of his jeans.

Ed pulled himself several feet, moving sluggishly across the shore, leaving shallow drag-marks upon the sand. Relief came as the man reached Daniel, then faded just as quickly as he lifted the boy from the waves and, rather than returning inland, began to slowly and deliberately march out to sea.

"Wait!" screamed Ed, frantically struggling to reach the foamy edge of the shifting tide. "What are you doing? Where are you going?"

The man paused once and turned his head. His eyes were no longer human. Instead, they were golden yellow in hue, with slit-like pupils running vertically down the center. They reminded Ed of the eyes of a serpent. "I am the master of your life, Ed Myers," he said, his voice hissing over the roar of the waves. "And of your son's, as well."

Then he turned and continued walking into the ocean. The crystal blue waves darkened, as if with inky shadow, and before long, the water had swallowed them whole.

"DANIEL!" Ed shrieked. But by the time he reached the foamy junction between sand and water, both were completely gone from sight.

The following afternoon found Ed at St. Alphonsus, the Catholic church he attended in Ocean Springs. He sat in one of the long pews near the altar, his thoughts alternating between prayer and troubled contemplation. He looked weary and disheveled in his jeans and Iowa State Cyclones shirt, as though he had not enjoyed a peaceful night's sleep for some time.

"Ah, Edward, my boy," came a familiar voice from behind him. Its crisp Irish accent echoed off the high ceiling of the sanctuary, amplifying it, causing it to sound like the booming voice of God Himself. "I thought I saw your scooter parked on the walkway outside."

The resonance of the speaker's words startled Ed at first. *He's followed me!* he thought, and then felt foolish for even letting it enter his mind. The lean, pony-tailed man with the snake tattoo was only a spectral player in his nightmares, not a real flesh-and-blood person.

He turned to see his priest standing in the center aisle. "Oh, Father White. Yes, I thought I'd come down today to spend a little time." He looked around the inner sanctum of the church. "This place comforts me. It's like a second home."

"The doors are always open." Father White was a tall, gaunt man, perhaps 70 years in age. His hair was silvery-white and balding on top. The elderly priest was a missionary from the Emerald Isle and a blessing to the parishioners of St. Alphonsus. He sat down in the pew ahead of Ed and turned around, his arm resting along the top of the seat. "Something's got you down in the dumps, Edward. You're not your normally exuberant self today. Now tell me, my boy, whatever is the matter? I'm here to listen if you'd like to talk."

Ed considered his words carefully before uttering them. "What do you make of dreams, Father?"

The priest shrugged. "Some are pure nonsense, I admit, while others may be meaningful in ways. The Bible is chocked full of such dreams. Jacob's slumber revealed the vision of a heavenward ladder laden with celestial angels. The dreams of the Pharaoh and Nebuchadnezzar were undecipherable to them, but clear to young Joseph and the prophet Daniel.

"And it is said that the apostle John's divine dreams prompted him to write the book of Revelations. So, yes, I believe that dreams can be insightful and even valuable at times; perhaps even messages from the Father Himself. But then there are others that are just plain rubbish, like if you're dreaming that you're at a big party with all your friends and you're parading around in your birthday suit."

Ed laughed. The good-humored sound rang strangely in his ears, having been absent for so long. Father White could always make him smile, even on the darkest of days. "But what about nightmares? If dreams are messages from God, couldn't nightmares be just the opposite? Couldn't they be orchestrated by Satan, in order to violate one's spirit, or even test their faith?"

The Irishman's smiling eyes grew suddenly somber. "Has ol' Lucifer been troubling you so? With nightmares and the like? You certainly look like a man who's been wrestling the horned-one in the dead of night."

"The Devil," said Ed. "Or worse."

For the next half hour, he told the parish priest of his recurring nightmares; of the icy crosswalk and endless beach stretching between him and his drowning son. And of the common denominator in both: the tall, thin man with the black hair and the serpent tattoo running down his right arm.

When he was finished, Father White regarded him thoughtfully. "Could these nightmares not be conjured by your own doubts and misgivings, Edward? Considering your recent separation, I'd say the thought of losing young Danny could explain your fear of abduction."

"You may be right. But it seems like something more than that. Something more... how do I put it... *sinister?*"

"Ah, the gentleman with the ponytail and the snake upon his arm," nodded Father White. "It could be your own inner feelings about your disability surfacing in the form of this unpleasant and contemptuous person. But, then, I am no psychiatrist...just a simple man of God, that's all."

"You are much more than that, Father," said Ed. "And some of what you say could be true. It's just that it's got me so on edge and Daniel is coming to stay with me this weekend."

"All will be fine, Edward," the priest assured him. "Just relax and enjoy your time with the boy. Ease your mind, and these nasty nightmares will likely fade and be gone."

"Hopefully you're right." But deep down inside, Ed Myers knew that the nightmares would continue until something disastrous took place. He didn't know why he felt that way, but he did, and it was a sensation of dread he simply couldn't shake.

The following Saturday night, Ed awoke in the middle of the night to a thunderous noise. Startled, he sat straight up in bed, his heart beating wildly.

Someone was pounding on the front door of his one-bedroom apartment. Loudly and insistently. Violently.

Ed flung his bedcovers aside and felt for his crutches in the darkness. When he located them, he left the bedroom and slowly started across the living room toward the front door. On the trundle bed in the corner, he saw the still form of Daniel, fast asleep, snuggled beneath his blanket.

The moment he reached the door, the frantic knocking ceased. Half angry, half frightened, he put his eye to the peephole in the center. "Who is it?" he demanded.

Ed was surprised to see his brother standing on the stoop. "It's Randy. Let me in, Eddie. It's important!"

After struggling with the deadbolt for a moment, Ed finally opened the door. "Randy? What are you doing—?"

Abruptly, Ed realized that he had made a terrible mistake. The form of his older brother shimmered before his eyes. Ed stumbled back several steps, feeling disoriented and scared. "You!" he gasped when he saw the image solidify into the tall figure of the man with the snake tattoo.

"Good evening, Ed," said the man in that rumbling baritone of his. "Mind if I come in and make myself at home?"

Ed began to push the door closed. Due to years of using mostly his arms and shoulders, Ed's upper body strength was superior to a normal man his age. But shove as he might, he failed to shut the intruder out. With a flex of his snake-adorned arm, the man muscled his way in. The door swung inward so forcefully that Ed was knocked off his feet. He careened into a wall and slid to the floor, his crutches spinning off into the darkness.

"Weakling," sneered the tall man with disgust.

"What do you want?"

"You know what I've come for. Or, rather, *who*." Then he entered the apartment and started across the living room for the trundle.

"No!" yelled Ed in horror. He felt along the floor for his crutches, but they were totally out of sight or reach.

"You have no choice in the matter!" hissed the tall man. Slowly, he turned his head. Ed watched, terrified, as his handsome features contorted into the hideous countenance of a snake. The yellow eyes with the narrow pupils glowed in the darkness like phosphorous. He laughed coarsely, his tongue, long and as pink as raw flesh, flickered, as though savoring the fallen man's panic and fear.

Ed watched as he bent down, gathered the sleeping child in his arms, and started back toward the door. As he passed, Ed reached out and grasped the man's calf, just above the leather sheath of his cowboy boot. Beneath the fabric of his jeans, the skin felt textured and rough, like the dry hide of a serpent.

Speechless, he could only sit on the floor and watch as the intruder made away with the most precious thing in Ed's life.

As the man stepped outside, the night seemed to close in around him like a concealing cloak, leaving only the pair of reptilian eyes hovering in inky blackness. "Oh, how rude of me," he rasped in a voice darker and more evil than anything that a book or movie could conjure. "Allow me to introduce myself. I am Legion. John Legion."

Then, with the scuffling of boot soles on concrete, he disappeared completely… causing Ed to awaken again, for real this time. He sat up and breathed deeply, trying to calm himself. His heart pounded so forcefully in his chest that, at first, he was certain he was on the verge of a heart attack.

In the darkness and the privacy of his bed, Ed prayed fervently and crossed himself. Then, shakily, he rose and reached for his crutches. They leaned against the wall next to the nightstand, where he had left them earlier that evening, after tucking Daniel into bed.

This was the worst one yet, he thought as he made his way out of the bedroom and headed toward the front door. *How much more can I take without going totally insane?*

When he reached the door, he found it securely locked. Ed closed his eyes, trying to calm his frazzled nerves. He stood there for a moment and let the afterimages of the nightmare fade. Then he made his way across the living room to the trundle bed.

He found Daniel where he had left him, snoozing peacefully, several hours before. The dark hair of his Puerto Rican heritage peeked just above the edge of the Toy Story blanket Ed had bought him for Christmas.

Ed's hand trembled as he reached out to tenderly stroke his head…feeling something warm and wet, he brought his hand up and saw his palm coated with blood.

· · ·

"Daniel!" he screamed. Terrified, he flung the blanket away. In his son's place lay a dead cat. Its glossy fur—seeping the blood of its slaughter—was the same coal black hue as Daniel's hair.

As the body of the cat limply tumbled to the carpeted floor, the glow of a streetlight shone from beyond the living room window. Where Daniel's six-year-old body had once slumbered, there was now only a pillow in a white pillowcase. Ed was shocked to discover that it was *his* pillow from *his* bed. The one he had been sleeping on during his most recent nightmare.

Mortified, Ed stared at the surface of the pillow. For, upon the pale fabric, was written a single word in the congealing blood of the dead cat.

And that word was LEGION.

Around eleven o'clock the next day, Ed returned to St. Alphonsus.

Father White was outside, sweeping the steps of the church, when Ed drove up in his motorized scooter. The priest paused, shocked by the paleness of Ed's face and the dark circles around his eyes.

"Faith and Begorrah, my boy!" he exclaimed, setting his broom aside. "You look ghastly!"

Ed's voice cracked as he spoke. "He took my son, Father."

"Who? Who has taken young Danny?"

"The man with the snake tattoo."

Father White studied him with concern. "Let's go into my study and talk, shall we? I'll brew a pot of coffee."

Ten minutes later, Ed sat and told the priest about the horrifying events of the night before; of his nightmare, followed by the awful realization that Daniel had been snatched from the trundle bed in the apartment's living room. He spoke of the police's suspicions and Maribel's fear, grief, and doubt. While no one openly said so, Ed had gotten the feeling that both the authorities and his estranged wife thought that *he* was somehow involved in his son's disappearance.

"Of course, that's absurd!" said the priest, pouring himself a cup of strong, black coffee. "Just as it is absurd that you believe that this man of your dreams is responsible."

"But he is responsible!" insisted Ed. "This monster... this *Legion...* somehow got into the apartment and... "

Father White's gaunt face drained of color and his eyes narrowed. "What did you say this fellow's name was?"

"Legion. He said his name was John Legion."

"Saints preserve us," the priest muttered. "Legion."

Suddenly, a passage from the Bible came to Ed, one he had not even considered until that moment. *Mark 5:9... And Jesus asked him, "What is thy name?" And he answered, saying, "My name is Legion, for we are many..."*

"No," said Ed, shaking his head. "That is impossible. He can't be... "

"But he is," Father White told him grimly. "One and the same."

Ed silently digested the revelation of who last night's intruder had truly been. "I've always believed in demons, but never thought that they could actually walk the earth."

"Oh, but they do," the priest said. "They are even worse than Lucifer in the Book of Job...going to and fro on the earth, and walking up and down upon it."

"Have you ever encountered one?" Ed asked him.

Father White was quiet for a long moment. Then he sat back in his chair and nodded. "Yes, I have, back in Ireland. And it was the very one who has victimized you these many nights. Legion... but in a different form." The old man shuddered at the memory. "It was a time when snakes once again slithered upon the hallowed earth of sweet Erin."

Ed hated to ask, but he had to. "Tell me about him."

"Legion is a demon of the vilest sort. A creature that feeds upon humiliation and doubt, fear and broken dreams. He seeks out the weak and toys with them, the same as a cat plays with a mouse before finally devouring it. Sometimes he appears in mortal flesh, sometimes in nightmares, like those you have suffered. As he told Christ, he is many. You've read of his numerous faces in books, both fiction and otherwise; Baal, Hitler, Flagg, Hastur, Leech. All are a direct extension of his evil."

"But if he is so powerful, how can he be defeated?"

"Defeat is not a word I would use," the priest told him. *"Cast away* or *put off* are more correct terms. Even Jesus, in all His glory, was unable to conquer his evil. He cast Legion out of the mad man and into a herd of pigs.

"The swine leapt to their deaths from a cliff, but was that the end of the demon? No. To this day, he continues to divide his time between hell and earth, tormenting the damned as well as the living."

"And he has taken Daniel."

"Yes," said Father White, solemnly. "But all is not lost. Legion has been known to use one to entrap another. I believe he is after you, first and foremost… because of your weakness and infirmity." The priest laughed with a twinkle in his eyes. "But he doesn't know you the way I do. You are not quite as helpless and defenseless as he believes you to be."

Ed shook his head despondently. "I'm not so sure of that."

Father White placed his hands upon Ed's shoulders. "Well, I am. And, when he contacts you, we shall be ready for him."

"Contacts me? You mean in another nightmare?"

"More than likely. Legion is known to enjoy bargaining with those he torments—like a nether-worldly con man, in a sense. He'll seek you out and use Danny as a pawn to satisfy his arrogance and iniquity. Legion will cast temptation in your path, a temptation so strong and alluring that only the strongest may resist. I honestly think you possess such strength, my friend."

"And if I should falter and accept his bargain?"

Father White's eyes were stern and steady. "Then Daniel shall be forever lost. And, spiritually, so will you."

Ed considered the possibility of betraying his son and told himself that it could never happen. But he was fully aware that he wasn't as strong and unbending as his friends and family thought he was. He had put on a brave face his entire life, standing fast against the injustice and disappointment that had threatened to bring him to the brink of depression and defeat time and time again. But, deep down inside, he knew that the weakness was there; cleverly hidden, but still there never the less.

The priest watched as Ed yawned in exhaustion. "Now, let's not discuss the matter for the moment. My couch is available, if you'd like to catch a few winks. I'm sure you were up all night long."

"Thank you," Ed said gratefully. "I may take you up on that." The thought of sleep was not at all appealing, considering the severity of the nightmares he had been subjected to lately, but if there was ever a haven for slumber, it was bound to be the leather sofa in Father White's office.

It seemed like he was out the moment his head rested against the padded arm of the couch. He experienced a long stretch of darkness. Then, gradually, sounds and smells came to him: the distant roar of waves and, closer, the *drip-drip-drip* of water hitting stone, as well as a dank and fishy odor.

Ed opened his eyes and found himself standing in the center of a small cave. The curved walls and ceiling were wet, as well as the water-smoothened floor. There were broad, saltwater puddles nearby occupied by starfish and a few other seashore creatures. He turned and looked through the mouth of the cave. A narrow strip of sandy beach, framed by boulders and marram grass could be seen and, further on, the ocean itself. Its vast blueness seemed to stretch into infinity.

"Daddy?"

Ed turned and saw Daniel in the shadows at the far end of the seaside cave. Barefooted, he stood looking frightened and miserable. His dark hair was plastered to his head and his pajamas were soaking wet.

"Daddy... I'm cold."

Ed wanted more than anything to go to him, to hold him and assure him that everything would be alright, but he couldn't. He seemed rooted to the spot; unable to move a single muscle. "Daniel, where are we?"

"At the cave," the boy told him. "Remember the one near the beach at West Ship Island? The one I wanted to explore... but we couldn't."

It pained Ed to even recall that bright afternoon nearly a year ago. Daniel had run up to him excitedly, pulling at his hand. "I found this neat cave, Daddy! Come on, let's go exploring!" Then the boy had looked him in the eyes, then at the crutches in the sand, and realized that what he asked was impossible. "Oh," was all he had said, but the disappointment in his dark eyes had spoken volumes. At that moment, Ed would have given anything—*anything*—to have been the sort of father who could play touch football or sprint down the beach flying a kite. The kind of father that Daniel deserved to have.

"Yes," Ed told him. "I know the place." He looked into the darkness beyond the boy. For some strange reason, it didn't appear as black and murky as before. Faintly, a flickering light, alternating between hues of red, yellow, and orange, seemed to generate from some point at the rear of the cave. And the cool dankness almost seemed to lift, replaced by a muggy, oppressive heat.

"He's here, Daddy," Daniel whispered fearfully. His lower lip trembled and his eyes brimmed with tears. "He said he was going to take me with him. Take me back to the Bad Place... to join the rest of his children."

"Don't worry," Ed told him. "I'm coming to get you, son."

Abruptly, Legion was there, standing behind the boy. His hands —glittering with smooth green scales and sporting black claws as sharp as razors—rested on the child's narrow shoulders. Those awful reptilian eyes gleamed with sly amusement. "Yes... do come, Ed. Tonight. After dark." That snake-like tongue, riddled with open sores and bleeding blisters, ran teasingly across ivory fangs. "We have business to discuss."

Then the cave lost its peculiar glow and grew pitch dark. Then Ed was sitting up in alarm, staring across the study at an antique clock sitting on an oaken bookshelf full of religious tomes. The time was only twenty minutes after the hour he had laid down to rest.

Father White was sitting at his desk, in the same spot he had been before. "Edward?"

"Father...I know where he is."

The elderly priest stood up solemnly. "Well, we didn't have to wait as long as we thought, did we?" He crossed the room to where an inspirational portrait hung in a gilded frame: Christ dangling from the cross, crucified, surrounded by angels, the Virgin Mary kneeling in prayer at his feet. White removed the painting. Behind it, was a wall safe. Silently, he worked the combination of the dial back and forth until it clicked. Then he opened the heavy metal door.

Ed watched as he brought out a small box of cherrywood trimmed in gold. "What is that?"

Father White sat on the edge of the couch and stared at the box for a long moment; respectfully, almost fearfully. "Within this box is a sacrament. A very special one. It was given to me by a bishop in Dublin many years ago." He lifted his eyes. They seemed haunted and scared. "This sacrament was only to be used in the direst of circumstances. I believe, in my heart and soul, that time has come."

"What significance does it have?"

"It brings one to *his* level," the priest told him, referring to Legion. "Without it, defeat is imminent. With it, you will have a fighting chance."

"*Me?*" said Ed with surprise. "You want *me* to use it?"

"It is your battle, Edward, not mine." He closed his eyes, his ancient hands cradling the box reverently. "Holy Father, forgive me! This action may be a sin in Your eyes, but if anyone other than myself deserves to partake of this, it is this young man."

"But how am I going to get there? To the cave near the beach?"

"I will take you where you need to go, Edward," Father White promised him. "But once the hour arrives, I'm afraid you must face the demon on your own."

. . .

It was late evening when Ed Myers and Father White made their way carefully down the dunes to the rocky place at the far end of West Ship Island Beach.

By the time they reached the mouth of the little cave, Ed was utterly exhausted. Even with the priest's help, it had been difficult moving through the loose drifts of fine white sand and thick tuffs of vegetation. The pads of his crutches kept sinking deeply into the dunes, making the journey nearly impossible. It took them close to thirty minutes to cover five hundred yards, but they finally made it.

"Sit down and rest, my boy," White suggested. Ed nodded quietly and sank to a sitting position beside a tall boulder, leaning his crutches beside him. The two looked off to the west. The brilliant orange and violet hues of the sunset blazed across the sky in streaks, like bold brushstrokes upon a canvas. The tableau would have seemed positively serene if it had not been for the dread of what was to take place there later that evening.

"Now what?" asked Ed with an edge to his voice. "Do I just sit here and wait for him to show up and finish me off?"

Father White crouched and stared him sternly in the eyes. "I know that you are tired, Edward, and feeling at the end of your rope. But you must hold fast. You must take steps… strong steps… to battle this fiend, face to face. Like I said before, you are Danny's only hope. You must not give up… for his sake."

"You're right. I'm sorry." Ed closed his eyes and breathed deeply. "Okay, what do we do next?"

The elderly priest opened the tiny wooden box. Inside was a single wafer of sacrament wrapped in a white velvet cloth. "I shall bless the Eucharist and administer it unto you." Both men clasped hands and prayed; Ed silently, while White softly spoke ancient Latin. Then the old man unwrapped the sacrament and laid it upon the flat of Ed's tongue. Afterward, he continued his prayer and ended it with familiar English. "In the name of the Father, the Son, and the Holy Ghost. Amen."

"Amen," said Ed, echoing the priest's humble reverence.

Father White remained before Ed for a few minutes. "How are you feeling, my boy?"

"Strange," Ed admitted. "I feel... exhilarated and weary... both at the same time." He looked at his priest with questioning eyes. "Is this some sort of narcotic?"

White smiled. "Something much more worthy than that. It's difficult to explain to a layman such as yourself. It is like rain upon the closed bulb of a flower; a flower that once slept, but now opens to its fullest and most glorious potential."

"I... I don't understand," mumbled Ed, feeling so sleepy that he could scarcely keep his eyes open.

"You shall," said Father White. He patted him affectionately on the shoulder, then turned to leave. "May God be with you, Ed Myers."

He awoke and stood. Unfaltering. Perfectly balanced.

Ed remained there, facing the entrance of the cave, marveling at the strength that coursed throughout his limbs. His legs remained erect, no longer surrendering to the weight of his upper body. He raised a hand before his eyes. There was no tremble to it at all. It was as steady as a stone.

Tentatively, he took one step, then another. Uncertainty was no longer a factor in his mind; he continued toward the cave, absent of the self-consciousness he had suffered during most of his life.

"Legion!" he called out. His voice was strong and firm, with no trace of a stammer or stutter. "I have come for my son."

Sinister laughter echoed from within the chasm. "Then what are you waiting for? Come and get him."

Ed walked through the opening and found himself in the cave he had dreamt of only hours before. The rear of the cave blazed with an intense light and heat that Ed could only describe as hellish. Sulfur, excrement, decay... every fetid stench imaginable originated from that infernal glow.

Standing before the light was John Legion. He was not in his serpentine form, but in the form of Ed's nightmares: tall and hand-some, his dark hair pulled into a ponytail, dressed in jeans and boots. Only the abominable tattoo on his right forearm and hand hinted at the being that lay concealed beneath mortal flesh and muscle.

Daniel crouched on the stone floor at Legion's feet. He looked small and sunken, his hands folded over his face, as if attempting to seal away the adversity he had endured during the past twenty-four hours... as well as the terror that was yet to come.

"Why have you taken him?" Ed demanded. "I need to know your purpose."

Legion laughed. "Purpose! I need no purpose, Ed. But if you insist on knowing..."

The tall man stepped over the child and sauntered toward his adversary. "Those of my kind, we cannot, shall we say, *procreate.* Therefore, if we desire offspring, we must simply take them. From the school yard, the mall, the crib late at night." A fiendish grin crossed his face. "You know all of those missing children you see on the backs of milk cartons and on the bulletin boards of supermar-kets? Half of them are now my sons and daughters. Waiting at home for dear old daddy to arrive. Of course, many don't survive. Many can't handle my form of...discipline. Those unfortunate souls end up back in your realm...homeless, insane, prone to drugs and drink. The next time you see a panhandler at a stop-light, begging for pocket change, ask him just how hot the flames of Hell can be."

"Daddy!" squealed Daniel, behind the mask of his hands. "Don't let him take me there!"

Ed stepped forward. "You're not going anywhere, baby."

Legion's smile grew as broad and bright as the unholy portal behind him. "Just look at you, Ed. So straight and strong. Feels good, doesn't it?"

Ed couldn't help but admit that he had never felt so powerful and confident during the entire span of his forty-six years.

"Yeah... you like it, don't you?" taunted Legion. "Well, it doesn't have to end. I possess the means to keep you this way. No more crutches, no more wheelchairs. Any woman you desire. That big journalism job you've always craved. At your fingertips...no questions asked."

"In exchange for?" Ed countered.

"Your son," rasped the beast that was John Legion. "A small price for perfection, wouldn't you say?"

Ed Myers had always wondered what he would have done if he had ever been offered such a wondrous gift; whether he would submit to human desire and weakness, or if he would make the hardest decision of his life and do the right thing.

At that moment, it surprised him at just how easy and uncomplicated such a monumental choice could be.

"Perfection be damned," said Ed. "Now step aside. I'm taking Daniel home."

It was at that moment that Legion's pleasant veneer crumbled, exposing the petulant fiend that lay beneath the surface. The countenance of the serpent revealed itself once again, those viperous eyes glowing as hot and scathing as the hell that burned behind him. "You're not going anywhere, Ed. And neither is your son."

Suddenly, and without warning, Legion lifted his right arm to full length. The tattooed flesh rippled and contorted, changing from fleshen art to hideous reality. Legion's arm evolved into the most horrifying serpent imaginable, the scaled hide seething with acidic oils and the fist-turned-head opening into a yawning maw akin to that of a rattlesnake. The curved fangs coursed with venom a thousand times more potent than that of an ordinary earthbound serpent. Arching back, it leered at the man standing before it with malicious glee, then swiftly struck.

Ed felt something within him react; something that he could have never described in words, but was sure of in spirit. He lashed out and caught the serpent beneath the head, holding its struggling length tightly, refusing to let go. At the same time, the serpent thrashed and writhed in panic and confusion. Its gleaming emerald scales blackened and its fangs shattered, falling from its mouth in brittle, impotent fragments.

Legion's face mirrored the terror of the serpent. "What... what is this?" he shrieked, sinking to his knees in fearful submission.

"Faith," Ed told him. "In all the centuries you've walked this earth, have you never felt its glory?"

A deafening chorus of torment and defeat, like a thousand agonized souls, filled the air as the thing called Legion lost its substance and began to dissolve in Ed's grasp. Then the portal at the rear of the cave burst into a luminance so brilliant and white-hot that everything—be it heaven, hell, or earth—was momentarily lost in its fury.

"Daddy? Daddy, wake up!"

Ed opened his eyes. He stared up at the rocky ceiling, aware that morning light was filtering in from the mouth of the little cave. "Daniel?"

The boy's small hands grasped his fingers tightly. "I'm here, Daddy. Are you okay?"

Feebly, Ed sat up. He no longer felt the strength he had experienced hours before. The ache of exhaustion settled into his muscles like a great weight, nearly pulling him down into a prone position once again. His head throbbed, his stomach rolled, and his limbs felt weaker than water.

"What... what happened?" he managed to say.

"I don't know," admitted Daniel. "I went to sleep on the bed in the living room and then I just woke up here... with you."

Ed thanked the Lord for small mercies. The boy remembered nothing of his awful ordeal.

"Do you see my crutches anywhere?" he asked.

"They're outside," said his son. "Beside that rock."

As Ed struggled to a sitting position, he watched as Daniel ran, barefooted, to the boulder, and returned carrying his crutches.

"Let's get out of here," Ed said as Daniel helped him to his feet. Ed took his time, feeling totally wiped out. Carefully, he made his way outside with his son walking beside him.

When they reached the warm sunlight and fresh sea spray of the Mississippi morning, Daniel pointed down at the ground. "Hey... look!"

Ed studied the tracks in the sand. They were the footprints of a man, leading from the boulder to the mouth of the cave. Prints that were of the same size and identical in shape to his own two feet.

He stared at the tracks for a long moment, expecting a twinge of regret to surface. But it never came.

"I wonder who they belong to," Daniel said.

"It doesn't matter," Ed replied. He swept the tracks away with the tips of his crutches until they could be seen no more. "All that matters is that you're okay."

Daniel smiled and slipped a hand affectionately through the crook of his father's arm. Slowly, they left the little cove and walked out onto the smooth, hard surface of the tide-washed beach.

When they reached the dunes, the boy seemed doubtful. "Do you think you'll be able to make it?"

Ed smiled at his son. "Piece of cake."

Together, they made their way up the sandy slopes toward the road, to see if Father White had come to take them home.

MIDNIGHT TIDE

DAVID GALLAGAN THOUGHT it was hilarious that Ginny's last name was Skipper.

Every time they crossed paths in Ponte Vedra or on the beach, he would throw up his hand and, in his best Bob Denver impression, call out "Hey, Skipper!" Ginny would reply with a hearty "How are you doing, Little Buddy?" The exchange broke the sixteen-year-old up every time. Ginny would have found the repetitive joke annoying if her young neighbor hadn't been such an endearing kid.

David was spending the summer in the bungalow to the left of Ginny's. The Gallagans were renting the three-roomer for a couple of weeks—just David, his eight-year-old brother, Todd, and their mother, Trish. If there was a Mister Gallagan, Ginny hadn't seen him around. She sort of got the impression that Trish was divorced, but had never really heard whether or not that was the case. The boys seemed well-adjusted and happy enough, playing on the beach or in the surf from daybreak to dusk.

Ginny's own bungalow wasn't much to look at, but it completely belonged to her and her husband, Allen. It sat upon a dune overlooking the Atlantic—a single-level structure with one bedroom, two front rooms, and beams and walls constructed of old Florida pine. The bungalow had been built in 1957 and its outer appearance was pretty much what you would expect from a beach house: creamy stucco walls and an abundance of eye-jarring aqua trim around the eaves, window shutters, and front door. In the scrubby yard, facing the ocean, was an iron and brass weathervane with a sailfish, leaping majestically on top. Ginny and Allen had affectionately named the fish "Sully" and they enjoyed seeing him whirl and lash as the ocean breeze sent him facing in one direction or another.

Ginny was there by herself that week in mid-June. Her daughter, Paige, who lived in the bungalow while they were away, was in New Jersey visiting relatives, which gave Ginny full reign of the beach house. The Skippers had planned to spend the week together, but a colleague of Allen's had been diagnosed with a heart ailment and, being a vascular surgeon, her husband had felt compelled to perform the procedure himself. He hoped to join her at Ponte Vedra on Friday. She was keeping her fingers crossed. At least then they could enjoy a long weekend together.

Ginny was no stranger to the medical profession herself. She was a registered nurse and had been for thirty-five years. She had experience in all areas of critical care, including the burn unit, and had even taught nursing. Currently, she was working with Allen, managing his office and involving herself in all aspects of pre- and post-operative patient care. Truthfully, Ginny had felt more than a little guilty taking off for an entire week, while Allen remained behind, attending to business as usual.

That Tuesday morning, Ginny was sitting in one of the bungalow's front rooms, tying her running shoes. The TV was on the early news. An anchorwoman was segueing from the national news to the local report. The top story concerned a missing couple, John and Sara Newbury, who had been honeymooning in St. Augustine. After several days of hearing nothing from her daughter, the bride's mother had contacted the authorities. The police had found their hotel room empty and their rental car abandoned near Crescent Beach. Absolutely no clues had been found as to what happened to them or their possible whereabouts. The news anchor ended the story with the possibility that the disappearance of the Newburys could be connected to four other missing couples that had suffered similar fates during the past two years, from Miami to Jacksonville, all of whom had never been located.

Ginny's two French bulldogs, Big Bad Boo and Bogie, were waiting anxiously at the front door, ready to go outside. "Alright, alright," she called, then stood up and turned off the television. The wedding photo of the honeymooning Newburys reminded Ginny uncomfortably of her own son, Justin, and his wife, Natasha. She could imagine how the other parents must feel with their children having vanished into thin air. The mystery of the chain of missing couples had the Florida Bureau of Investigation wondering if there was a particularly crafty serial killer at work along the state's eastern coast.

The moment Ginny opened the door, the red fawn and tiger bindle burst into the morning sunlight. They barked playfully as they bounded through the sawgrass and headed down the dune toward the beach. Ginny smiled to herself as they plowed into a sand castle the Gallagan boys were currently constructing. David and Todd moaned in faux disgust, but ended up wrestling with the two bulldogs in the sand.

Ginny stretched and prepared for her morning run down the beach. She was a tall woman of average weight, with unruly silver-brown hair that fell slightly below her shoulders. She was in her mid-fifties and—despite a few wrinkles—had retained her youthful beauty, along with several engaging dimples when she smiled. She had long, athletic legs and loved to run. Ginny usually ran or walked at least five miles a day and had won many half marathons at Disney World and New York City.

"Good morning, Sully," she called out as she trotted past the weather vane. The sailfish shifted slightly, its rapier-like nose pointing due south.

As Ginny hit the beach and began to run, she waved at David. "Morning, Gallagan, Little Buddy!"

David laughed and pushed Bogie off him. "Morning, Skipper... my BIG old buddy!"

"Hey, I kind of resent that," Ginny said, chuckling.

David's mirth increased, much to his little brother's annoyance. "Hey, it's not that funny," Todd told him.

"Sure it is!" said David. "Come on. Let's get back to this castle. I want to finish it before lunchtime."

As the boys began to repair the damage the two bulldogs had wrought, Big Bad Boo and Bogie took off after their mistress. Ginny was gathering steam and increasing her pace. She glanced back to see that Bogie had stopped to check out a beached jellyfish. "Un-uh, sweetie," she called back. "Get away from that or you might get stung. Those things can hurt you as much when they're dead as when they're alive." They had experienced an increasing epidemic of dead jellyfish on Ponte Vedra Beach lately, but there was really nothing that could be done about it.

Ginny transferred her sunglasses from the top of her head to the bridge of her nose, cutting the glare of the eastern sun. The tide had packed the sand to a satisfying hardness and her traction was excellent. She took off southward, down the beach. She usually ran to Palm Valley and back, which made for a good two-mile sprint. After that, Ginny would return to the bungalow for a bite of breakfast, if she felt like it. Paige never kept anything in the cabinets that Ginny liked. Sometimes she'd run down to the local market and pick up some Froot Loops or those little powdered donuts, but normally she just opted for a big lunch.

As she approached the bungalow that sat to the right of Ginny's, she couldn't help but glance at the weathered steps that wound up the dune to the pale blue and coral structure. This beach house was a little bigger than the one she and Allen had purchased and probably demanded a pretty penny from those who chose to rent it. It was currently occupied by a man named Hargrove, although Ginny had only seen him from a distance. She knew nothing about him, except for what the clerk at the store had told her. She had said Hargrove was a strange bird, both in habits and appearance.

As chance had it, Ginny was surprised to find him sitting on the bottom step, dressed in khaki shorts, a white collarless shirt, and sandals. He was reading a Stephen King novel, which made Ginny grin. She, too, had bought the master's latest book, but hadn't had a chance to dig into it.

"Hi," she said, slowing up. "I'm your next-door neighbor, Ginny Skipper."

"Glad to meet you," he said, lifting his face from the book. "My name is Jason Hargrove."

Ginny stopped dead in her tracts and stared for a long moment. She shouldn't have been all that startled. After all, she had seen someone with a prosthetic face before, during her time in the ER. But that patient's face had been more of a featureless mask, hiding the ravages of a particularly destructive fungus. Jason Hargrove's prosthesis was a little more sophisticated. The half-mask sported a glass eye that matched the same azure blue of his real one, half a nose, cheekbone, and a set of upper and lower lips that were curled into a lazy sort of boyish smile. The illusion that was intended was far from perfect, though. The right side of the man's face was tanned and handsome, while the false side was several shades paler and unnervingly unreal, much like the face of a child's doll. In an odd way, he sort of reminded her of Two-Face in the old Batman comics.

"Alarming, aren't I?" he asked, setting his book down.

"I apologize if I seem rude," Ginny said quickly. Despite her discomfort, she smiled and looked him square in his good eye. "It's not like I haven't seen a facial prosthesis before."

Hargrove's left eyebrow raised. "Oh, really? Do you work in the medical profession?"

"Yes. I'm a registered nurse," she said.

A spark of interest seemed to ignite in his one good eye. "An RN? That's interesting. I was once a doctor myself." He pointed to the right side of his face. "Before this."

"Excuse me for asking, but what happened to you?"

"Cancer," he said. "A particularly stubborn form of melanoma. I was lucky that I ended up with what I have left. I lost plenty, though. My wife, my family, my career. I may not look it, but I was one of the most successful plastic surgeons in Tallahassee at one time."

Ginny simply nodded. She didn't know quite how to respond.

"Well, I'd best get back to my book," he said, giving her an easy way out of an awkward situation.

"And I to my morning run," she replied. "It was nice meeting you, Dr. Hargrove."

"Jason," he insisted. Again, that peculiar sparkle seemed to gleam in his right eye.

"You can just call me Ginny." Then, with a friendly wave, she was off.

Ginny ran past Hargrove's sailboat, which was tethered to an iron post near the shoreline. She had seen him take it out the day before, late in the evening when it was nearly dark. A strange time to go sailing, she had thought at the time.

As she distanced herself from the half-faced man, she couldn't help but breathe a sigh of relief. She could handle adverse physical conditions better than most professionals she worked with, but it was simply the styling of the prosthesis that gave her the creeps, or so she supposed.

But as she got farther into her run, Ginny knew that it was more than Hargrove's half-mask that was disturbing. There was something about the man that bothered her. Maybe it was the way he had practically lit up when she mentioned she was a nurse. But hopefully that was only professional curiosity on his part and nothing more.

That night, Ginny had the worst nightmare of her entire life.

She found herself running—not on the beach or the highway—but on a deserted city street. It was night and only the halogen glow of a few random streetlights illuminated her way. But she wasn't running for the fun of it. Her speed was fueled by desperation and fear.

Up ahead, Ginny saw a dark van parked at the curb. The back doors swung open. A form in black sweats and a hooded jacket was loading two people into the back: a man and woman bound hand and foot with silver duct tape and gagged with filthy rags. As Ginny grew nearer, she was shocked to see that the couple was Justin and his Ukrainian bride, Natasha. They struggled weakly, but seemed to be succumbing to some powerful drug.

"No!" she screamed. As she grew nearer, she was alarmed to find that her other five children—Victoria, Stewart, Nathan, Jonathan, and Paige—were also prisoners in the van. They sat around the inner walls, all bound and gagged. It was like some family reunion gone horribly wrong.

A moment later, Ginny was there. During her frantic sprint, all she had wanted was to reach her babies. But now that she was at the back bumper of the vehicle, a strange sense of inner confusion gripped her. She was at a loss as to what she should do next.

The man in the black sweat suit turned and faced her. Ginny was stunned to find that he wore one of those transparent plastic Halloween masks–the kind that is garishly painted with over exaggerated eyebrows and lips, but gives a hint of the true face underneath. But there was something terribly wrong. Half of the face, complete with one bright blue eye, was visible behind the mask, but the other half seemed like some dark and bottomless void. The eyehole was empty. There was no eyeball there at all.

The abductor handed her two items. "Here. Hold these."

Obediently, Ginny reached out and took a roll of duct tape and an empty syringe.

"Let's go." The man began to close the doors of the van. As they swung shut, the eyes of her children regarded her with shock and accusation. Paige's tearful eyes pleaded with her, but Ginny's heart felt like a cold stone in her chest. Her daughter's terror seemed to have absolutely no effect on her.

When the doors were secure, the abductor walked around to the driver's side, while Ginny climbed into the passenger seat. *What the hell is wrong with me?* she wondered. *What sort of hold would this man have over me that would make me betray my own children?*

The man started the van and then looked over at her with his one good eye. "One of them should do nicely," he said. Then, together, they headed down the deserted street into the darkness.

Ginny awoke with a shuddering gasp of alarm. She sat up in bed, trembling, staring into the darkness. She had been crying in her sleep. Tears filled her eyes and ran down her cheeks. She glanced over at the digital alarm on the nightstand. It read 11:52.

One of the Frenchies stirred where he snoozed at the foot of the bed. Big Bad Boo lifted his head sleepily and whimpered. Bogie lay still, exhausted from his romp on the beach.

Ginny reached down and ran a hand gently down the dog's back. "It's okay, baby. Just a nightmare. Back to sleep now."

Boo didn't argue. A few seconds later, he had settled down and was slumbering once again.

Ginny climbed out of bed and left the bedroom. After a trip to the bathroom, she made her way through the dark bungalow. The only light in the house was the trace of moonlight filtering through the slits of the window blinds. Quietly, she opened the front door and looked out onto the seashore. The moon was full and bright that night. It cast a silvery glow upon the rolling waves and the smooth, sandy strip of the beach.

She stepped outside, neglecting to slip on her flip-flops. Barefooted and dressed in only shorts and a t-shirt, Ginny made her way down the slope of the dune to the beach. When she got there, she stood there for a long moment, her eyes closed, letting the ocean breeze wash over her. She drank in the salty air and let the roar of the approaching tide fill her ears, drowning out all other noise.

The details of the nightmare threaten to resurface, but she pushed them back into that dark place where ugly dreams fade to upon wakening. *What caused me to dream that?* she wondered. Had it been the constant coverage of the honeymooners' disappearance in

St. Augustine? And maybe her disturbing introduction to Jason Hargrove had played a part in it, too. Whatever had conjured such an awful dreamscape, Ginny hoped that she never had to experience it again. Standing there on the beach, she got a wild impulse to go back to the bungalow, find her cell phone, and call every one of her children. But that would be silly. She knew they were safe and sleeping. There was no need to wake them up for the sake of her own foolish nightmare.

Ginny walked to the edge of the surf, careful not to step on a sharp shell or, heaven forbid, one of those beached jellyfish. She stood with her feet in the water for a long moment, relishing the feel of the cool water. The ebb and flow of the midnight tide seemed to lull her back into a state of relaxation. The alarm she had felt a few minutes ago had drifted away.

Then it returned as something washed up from out of the ocean and clung to the instep of her left foot.

Startled, she looked down, expecting to see a jellyfish there. Instead, it was something she wasn't expecting at all. Something that sent a spike of adrenalin and horror surging throughout her.

It was a face. The flaccid skin of a human face, lying upon her naked foot. She stared down at it for a moment, unable to comprehend the reality of its presence at first. It looked as if it had been traced out and extracted from high in the scalp, just forward of the ears, and down along the jawline. The nose and lips were pale and bloated; and blue with lack of blood. The most horrifying feature was the twin eye sockets, both empty and devoid of the organs they had once framed.

Then the tide rolled in once more and reclaimed it.

Ginny jumped backward in alarm. She stood there, arms folded across her chest for a while, trying to slow her hammering heartbeat. *Was that for real?* she asked herself. *Did I really see what I thought I saw? Or was it some aftereffect of that stupid nightmare?*

She stood there in indecision for a moment longer, then walked to the edge of the water, searching for that disembodied face. But she found no trace of it. Had it been for real, or just a figment of her imagination? It had certainly felt real, plastered upon the instep of her foot.

Shaken, Ginny turned away from the tide. The Gallagans' bungalow was dark, but Hargrove's windows were still lit. She knew she shouldn't feel the way she felt about the man, but he gave her the creeps.

She made her way back up the slope of the dune, through the sawgrass, to her own bungalow. Ginny cast an uncertain glance back toward the rolling whitecaps of the tide, then closed the door. And, although she didn't know exactly why, she did something she had never felt the need to do before. She locked and bolted her door. Then she went back to bed.

Ginny's run the next morning was an introspective one. Normally she ran for exercise or fun, but this time it was to clear her head and reflect on the disturbing incidents of the night before.

The nightmare still lingered in her mind, although some of the finer details had faded following her awakening. She still recalled her abducted children in the van and the man with the transparent Halloween mask. But most of all, Ginny remembered her willingness to conspire with the abductor. She supposed that was the worst aspect of the dream—that she would purposely put her flesh and blood, or anyone else for that matter, in physical danger.

And then there was the face in the tide. In the glow of moonlight, the disembodied face had seemed horrifying and more than a little surreal. But now, in broad daylight, it all seemed silly and improbable. Last night she had even considered calling the police. That didn't seem like an option at all now. Ginny was beginning to believe that she had imagined the whole episode. It had seemed so damned *real* though... the way the flesh had shimmered in the currents of the tide, the way it had felt, cold and flaccid, plastered to the top of her foot.

Ginny was almost back at the bungalow when she heard someone call her name. She saw David Gallagan jumping up and down waving his hands. His little brother was sitting in the sand beside the surf. From a distance, it looked as though Todd was crying.

What happened? she wondered.

Ginny poured on the speed and got there ten seconds later. "What's wrong, David?"

"Todd stepped on a jellyfish," said the teenager. It was clear to see that David was both excited and scared half out of his wits. "I told him to wear his sandals, but, no, he had to act like a stupid little kid!"

"I'm not stupid!" Todd yelled at him. He looked up at the woman tearfully. "It hurts, Ginny! It hurts bad!"

Ginny knelt down. "Just calm down, Todd. Let me take a look at it."

The jellyfish had beached that morning more than likely and still had a little life left in it. Two of its tentacles were wrapped around the eight-year-old's toes and the instep of his right foot. The tentacles' stinging cells—nematocysts—were already injecting its toxins into the boy's flesh. The skin beneath the tentacles was becoming red and inflamed.

"I've heard that it helps if you, well, pee on it," said David.

"Actually, urine doesn't help at all," Ginny told him. "Besides, do you want to pee on your brother's foot?"

David's face reddened in embarrassment. "Heck, no!"

"Yeech!" exclaimed Todd in horror.

Ginny thought about it for a moment. "Run up to my bungalow to the kitchen. There's a bottle of vinegar in the cabinet beside the sink. And bring a fork, too, so I can lift these tentacles off."

"Gotcha!" said the teen. Then he was running up the dune toward the beach house.

"Everything's going to be okay, Todd," Ginny assured him. "Where's your mom?"

"She had to drive into Jacksonville for a dentist appointment," he told her. "It's burning real bad!"

"I know, sweetheart. We'll have you feeling better in just a minute, okay?"

Suddenly, a shadow fell across them both. "What's going on here?"

Ginny turned and looked up to see Jason Hargrove standing a few feet away. His sudden appearance startled her, although she couldn't imagine why. She supposed she was still jumpy from the night before.

"Todd stepped on a jellyfish," she told him.

Hargrove nodded grimly. "Nasty things, aren't they?"

Ginny turned to find the eight-year-old boy staring at the man. "Hey, why is he wearing a mask?"

She leaned in close to the boy and softly whispered to him. "Dr. Hargrove had a serious illness that damaged part of his face. He has to wear the mask to hide it." She hoped the man wouldn't overhear, but he did.

"Don't worry," Hargrove told them. "I know it's terribly disturbing. Children don't always understand. I'm use to their stares by now."

Ginny felt it was best to steer away from the subject of Hargrove's prosthesis as quickly as possible. "Doctor, would you like to take a look at the wound?" she asked, more out of professional courtesy than anything else.

Hargrove looked uncomfortable. "I no longer practice medicine," he told her. "And my malpractice insurance has lapsed."

Ginny was angered by the man's response. She hadn't asked the former plastic surgeon to do a boob job on the spot. "I'll take care of it myself."

"I'm sorry, but I…"

"I said I'll attend to it. Don't concern yourself."

Soon, David was back with the bottle of white vinegar and a fork from the silverware drawer. When he saw Jason Hargrove's face, his eyes widened a bit. He looked down at Ginny, who shook her head slightly, warning him to make no comment.

Ginny uncapped the vinegar and poured it liberally over Todd's foot. "This should help neutralize the poison." Then she took the fork and began to gently lift the tentacles from around the boy's foot and toes.

"You have a capable hand, Nurse Ginny," said Hargrove from over her shoulder.

Ginny was still irked at his unwillingness to help Todd, so she thought she'd shake him up a little. "You're not coming on to me, are you, Doctor?"

"Why, certainly not!" stammered Hargrove. She looked up to see that his half-face had flushed bright red with embarrassment.

"I was only joking," she told him.

"Yes, of course," he said. "That was very... funny."

She couldn't tell for sure, but there seemed to be an edge of disdain in his voice.

Soon, Ginny had unwound all the tentacles from around Todd's foot and removed all remaining barbs and stinging cells. She again poured vinegar over the length of the boy's foot. The inflammation didn't look quite so red and angry now. "Feel any better?"

"Yeah," said Todd. "It doesn't sting as much now."

"David, help me get him up to the house and I'll bandage him up," Ginny told him. "When your mother gets back, she can take him to the emergency room, just to be on the safe side."

"Thanks for your help, Ginny," said the boy, obviously relieved. "You're a lifesaver."

As Ginny stood up, she looked over at Jason Hargrove. She was disturbed to find that he was not looking at her or Todd, but directly at David Gallagan. He practically *stared* at the boy. There was a peculiar look on the doctor's partial face that she couldn't quite identify.

"I feel cold," complained Todd. "And kinda sick to my stomach."

"Come on, David," she said. "Let's get him inside."

A moment later, she and David had Todd's arms around their shoulders, helping him up the slope of the dune to Ginny's bungalow. As they reached the door, she glanced back and saw Hargrove still standing there, watching David's every move. At first, she figured him for some sort of child molester who had a fetish for young boys, but that wasn't it. The expression was not one of desire or lust. As she attempted to analyze it, an entirely different word came to mind.

Covet.

But what would he possibly want from David? His youth? His good looks?

David seemed to be aware of the attention the man was giving him, too. "What a freakazoid!"

"I'm beginning to believe you're right," said Ginny as they carried Todd inside and closed the door.

Late Thursday night, Ginny dragged home, exhausted and worried half to death. It was as though her nightmare was somehow coming true.

For most of the day, David Gallagan had been missing. Ginny had seen him walking along the beach early that morning, looking alone and bored without his little brother tagging along. By the time she had returned at noon from running a few errands in Ponte Vedra, the boy's mother was knocking at her door, trying to locate his whereabouts. Together, they had searched the beach all the way to Palm Valley and back, and then northward to Jacksonville Beach. They had found no sign of him. It was then that Trish Gallagan had begun to grow hysterical. It wasn't like David to wander off for hours at a time. It was as though a wave had rolled in and carried him away, erasing all trace of him.

Ginny, Trish, and Todd had driven into Ponte Vedra and looked there. Still, no one had seen a sign of him. By five o'clock in the afternoon, they had ended up at the police station and filed a missing person report. The officer in charge had seemed annoyingly unconcerned about the matter, telling them it was common for teenagers to wander off and lose track of time; that maybe David had joined up with some friends or, heaven forbid, ran away from home. Trish had lashed into him angrily, ending up in tears, and

Ginny had driven her and Todd home. The police had promised that they would begin searching for the boy in the morning if he didn't turn up by then, but Ginny had a bad feeling that he wouldn't. Something had happened to the boy on Point Vedra Beach, she was certain of it.

After dropping the Gallagans off at their bungalow, Ginny had driven to the ranger station at the edge of the wildlife preserve across the highway from their beach houses. She told the ranger on duty of David's disappearance, on the off-chance that he may have wandered onto the preserve. The ranger had assured her that he would keep an eye out for him. After leaving, Ginny had driven around some more, but still she could find no sign of the boy.

It was a quarter till ten when she finally unlocked the bungalow door and walked in to find the Frenchies happy to see her. She hurriedly fed them, then opened a bag of chips, which she knew would probably serve as her supper. She also poured herself a Fresca. Normally Ginny mixed it with vodka, but that night she really didn't feel like indulging in her favorite drink, afraid that she might get a call about David's whereabouts and have to drive again.

She was turning on the TV, preparing to watch the local news, when her cell phone rang. Ginny was relieved to discover that it was her husband, Allen.

"I thought I'd drive on out and join you tonight," he said. "I know it's late, but, hell, I miss my Great She."

"Yes, please come on," she told him, sounding more frazzled than she intended to. "I don't feel like I want to be here alone tonight."

"What's the matter, Ginny? Is something wrong?"

She told him about David's disappearance and her fruitless search for the boy.

"I'll be there in half an hour," he assured her. "We'll get a good night's sleep, then get up early in the morning and look some more. Don't worry. He'll turn up somewhere."

"Thanks," she said. "Hurry on, will you?"

"I'm grabbing my keys now. I love you."

"I love you, too. Be careful."

Ginny hung up and laid her phone on the kitchen counter. The nightly news was coming on and she wanted to watch it while she snacked. She was just entering the living room when the front door opened. *Damn,* she thought, her heart leaping. *I am so tired, I forgot to lock it!*

For some reason, she wasn't at all surprised to find Jason Hargrove walking through the doorway.

"What do you want?" she demanded, feeling outrage and fear in light of his intrusion.

Hargrove closed the door behind him. "You really should lock your doors, Ginny. You never know who might barge in on you."

"I asked you... *what do you want?*"

That odd half-smile crossed the right side of the man's face, looking more sinister than silly now. "I am in need of your assistance, Nurse Skipper. For an important procedure tonight."

Behind her, on the television, a breaking story was being reported. The body of one of the missing honeymooners had been discovered in a sandy grave near Daytona Beach. Although the police refused to confirm it, inside sources claimed that the flesh of the man's face had been removed.

Suddenly, she knew what was going on. Jason Hargrove hadn't been coveting David's youth or good looks the day before.

He had been coveting his face.

"Oh my God! You've got David!"

Hargrove lifted his right hand from his side and leveled a 9mm pistol at her. "Please, come along. I can make this very difficult for you, if you choose to make it so."

At that moment, Big Bad Boo and Bogie padded into the room and growled, sensing the man's hostility toward their mistress.

"Please take them into the bedroom and shut the door," he told her. "I'd hate to have to harm your precious Frenchies."

Ginny could tell by the look in his good eye that he wasn't lying. "Come on, guys," she said softly, taking them by the collars. Soon they were in the bedroom with the door closed securely.

The doctor motioned with the barrel of his gun. "Shall we go?"

Ginny knew nothing else to do but to do as he said. If she attempted to escape or reach her cell phone in the kitchen, he would surely gun her down. Silently, she nodded.

Together, they left the bungalow and, in the moonlight, made their way down the dune to the beach. Once there, they began the short walk to Hargrove's beach house.

"So the face in the tide was your doing?" she asked on the way.

"What do you mean?" His voice came from a few feet behind her.

"I went for a walk Tuesday night, around midnight. A human face washed up in the tide. I thought I'd imagined it, but now I know it was for real."

Jason Hargrove laughed grimly. "I thought I'd disposed of it better than that. I supposed something got into the bag I dumped from my boat. A shark or dolphin perhaps." He was silent for a moment, then he continued. "It was an unacceptable specimen. Totally unsuitable for my needs. When I first saw it, it seemed fine. But after I extracted it from the donor, I found the first traces of melanoma on the left cheek. And I certainly didn't want to deal with that again. A wasted effort from the beginning."

"And the woman? You always take them in pairs."

"Merely a temporary assistant," Hargrove told her. "Of course, few of them wanted to cooperate. It took much *conditioning*... to get them to do what I needed them to do. But now I know that I was going about it all wrong. I didn't need a novice. I needed someone who knew what they were doing. Someone like you."

"And what makes you think I'm going to cooperate?"

"Because if you don't, I'll kill you and the boy," he told her in a flat, matter-of-fact tone that chilled Ginny to the bone. "And after that, I'll go to the Gallagan bungalow and kill the woman and her son. It wouldn't be the first time that innocents have suffered in order to order to fill my needs."

Ginny said nothing else. The man was crazy. She knew without a doubt that he was capable of doing exactly what he promised.

Soon, they were mounting the steps to Hargrove's rental house.

The front part of the house was dark. The only light seemed to come from the rear of the bungalow.

"Please proceed to the back bedroom and we shall begin," the man told her. When she hesitated, Ginny felt the muzzle of the pistol jab her in the small of the back. "I said to *proceed.*"

It was at that moment that Ginny knew that she must do everything in her power to put Hargrove at ease and make him believe she was a willing assistant to his fiendish plans. If she didn't prove her loyalty and gain his confidence, she would surely die.

When she stepped into the rear bedroom of the beach house, she definitely knew that the man was insane. The room had been turned into a makeshift operation room, but of a very bizarre kind. The place reeked of disinfectant. At one side was a padded chair—a dentist's chair, to be exact—with a large mirror and a bank of soft halogen lights set at an angle from the ceiling. On a pivoting arm attached to the chair was a stainless-steel tray of scalpels, surgical instruments, and suturing materials. Although it seemed utterly impossible to Ginny at the moment, it looked as though it had been orchestrated for someone to operate on *themself.*

On the opposite side of the room was a twin bed with David Gallagan tied securely in place with nylon rope. An IV was hooked up to him and a steady drip seemed to keep the teenager in a state of strong sedation. Seeing him lying there, imprisoned both physically and chemically, was disturbing, but even more so was the fact that surgical guidelines had been traced around the circumference of his face in black ink. A roadmap for the grisly work to come.

As Ginny moved to the center of the room, Hargrove locked the bedroom door, then made his way to the chair, keeping the muzzle of the 9mm aimed directly at his assistant at all times. "I've already prepared the donor for the procedure," he said rather clinically.

"His name is David!" Ginny snapped, feeling her anger rise.

Jason Hargrove's half-face blazed bright red with outrage. "Silence! The *donor's* identity is not crucial at this point!" It was obvious that he was of the variety of serial killer who wished to distance himself from the fact that his victims were actual human beings. Ginny remembered a line from Thomas Harris's *Silence of the Lambs.* "It puts the lotion on its skin."

Ginny breathed deeply and tried to control her own emotions. *You're going to screw up big-time, if you don't make like the perfect assistant. You'll end up like those other poor girls.*

"I apologize, Doctor," she said as evenly as possible. "This... donor... means nothing to me. I was getting sick and tired of him hanging around anyway... making those stupid jokes."

Hargrove studied her for a moment, then nodded. "Very well, Nurse Skipper. Shall we continue?"

Ginny stared impassively into his half-and-half face, refusing to look at the gun in his hand, but knowing it was there, nonetheless. "Yes. Just tell me what I need to do."

The plastic surgeon seemed pleased to have such a cooperative assistant for a change. "Good. First, I shall prepare myself, then we will extract the donor material for the transplant."

Ginny glanced over at the unconscious teenager. She used to regard David as a "fresh-faced young man", but now that innocent phrase had a horribly sinister connotation to it.

Hargrove removed his shirt, unbuttoning it with one hand, and then carefully climbed into the dentist chair. "I must inform you, I am ambidextrous. I can operate—or fire a gun—with either hand."

Ginny nodded, feeling her heart begin to race. "I understand."

The doctor settled into his seat. "Now, first, we must deaden the nerves around the damaged area. Please, if you will, remove my prosthesis."

Ginny's resolve faltered for a moment. "I... I'm not sure..."

The metallic click of the 9mm's hammer being thumbed back rang crisply in her ears. "I said... *remove my face.*"

She breathed in deeply, stepped forward, and gently lifted the prosthesis away. The plastic half-mask hid a horror she had never witnessed, even on her worse night in the ER. The left side of Jason Hargrove's face was a dried-up and dead crater of sunken flesh and exposed bone. The eye socket was a deep, puckered hole and from forehead to jaw, most of the flesh had been eaten away by cancer or surgically removed to prevent the spreading of the melanoma. The nasal cavity was exposed, and the upper and lower jaws grinned ghoulishly at her, the teeth bleached as white as those of the opposite side.

Hargrove stared at her with his one surviving eye. "Now you see why success is imperative. Why sacrifices must be made to correct this... abomination."

Ginny felt dizzy and disoriented, as though she might faint. "Yes, I see," she muttered.

"Please position the surgical tray before me."

Grimly, she did as he said, swinging the jointed steel arm with the tray of scalpels, syringes, and suturing hooks on the end, until it was directly in front of him. He switched the pistol to his left hand, keeping it constantly leveled at Ginny's stomach. Then Hargrove took a Sharpie marker from the tray and, studying his ruined face in the mirror, began to mark the flesh around the left side with small X's.

"I am marking the spots in which you shall inject a solution of Lidocaine mixed with epinephrine to decrease the amount of bleeding that might occur. Each injection will be a dose of five ccs. As you can see, I have plenty on hand."

Ginny looked at the syringe that he indicated. It was one of the largest used by physicians and surgeons—60 ccs—and this one was filled to capacity. The syringe held enough Lidocaine to numb half an elephant.

"Please, take the syringe and proceed," he instructed. Hargrove laid his head back, but extended the gun until the muzzle pressed firmly against Ginny's abdomen. "I do have your complete loyalty, don't I, Nurse?"

"Yes, Doctor," she said.

Hargrove nodded and breathed in deeply, relaxing. Ginny began to make the 5 cc injections, starting above the left eye socket. The procedure was in vain, though. Most of the flesh she attempted to inject was dead and dry, totally devoid of live nerve endings. It was like putting a Band-Aid on a chunk of raw hamburger... totally pointless. But such were the delusions of the disfigured plastic surgeon that he thought there was still a chance of correcting the devastation of his facial cancer.

As she worked, the man spoke to her, as though attempting to rationalize his madness. "This is my sixth attempt, you know. All the others met with one disaster or another. Mostly flaws in the transplant material or the resistance of the assistants to complete the task. But this shall be a success. The donor is in his prime. We shall meld perfectly."

Oh God, this man is a monster! Ginny's mind raced, trying to find some way to alter the chain of events that was transpiring. She had to figure out some route of escape that didn't involve the deaths of her and David... and the rest of the Gallagans for that matter. And then there was Allen to consider. He would arrive at the bungalow at any minute. If he found her gone and the Frenchies locked in the bedroom, he would assume the worst. And he would come looking for her.

Ginny almost lost it at that point, but she took a deep breath and continued with the third injection. That would leave 45 ccs of Lidocaine-ten times more than was actually needed for such a procedure.

Abruptly, an idea came to her, but to attempt it would be putting her life in peril. She knew she had no choice. Ginny had to take the chance.

"Please lean forward, Doctor," she requested without a shred of emotion in her voice.

"Excuse me?"

"Have you forgotten that we must deaden the sternocleidomastoid and trapezius muscles of your neck?" she asked him. "If we don't...well, the pain could prove to be debilitating."

Hargrove considered it and then nodded. "Yes... yes, you are absolutely right." He leaned forward slightly, exposing the back of his neck.

Ginny Skipper stared at the column of flesh for a long moment. "You know, Doctor," she said in scarcely a whisper. "You were right.

I am different from all those other assistants. I definitely know what I'm doing."

Then, with a steady hand born of some inner reserve of courage she never knew she possessed, Ginny inserted the needle of the syringe between the fourth and fifth cervical vertebrae, pumping the entire contents of the syringe into Jason Hargrove's spinal cord.

She knew that she was gambling with her life. She had no idea if the large dose of Lidocaine would have the same effect as the fentanyl or meperidine used in customary epidurals. Ginny's stomach muscles tightened, preparing for the report of the pistol and the impact of the bullet tunneling through muscle and internal organs. Perhaps the projectile might even shatter the bones of her own spinal column, leaving her crippled, if not dead.

But the blast from the pistol never came. The drug worked swiftly. Hargrove slumped forward limply, his head resting upon the tray of surgical tools. "You... you traitor!" he rasped harshly, unable to move from the neck down.

Ginny carefully took the gun from his rubbery fingers and set it aside. "You better believe it."

Exhausted, she went to David and checked his vitals. They were normal. She considered cutting off the IV drip, but decided to let him awaken far from this hellish operating room. She didn't want him coming to and seeing exactly what Dr. Hargrove had intended for him.

Ginny left the beach house and, with effort, made her way down the wooden steps to the beach below. The sand seemed strangely unstable beneath her feet and, for one frightening moment, she felt as though it might change into quicksand and consume her entirely.

"Ginny!" a familiar voice called from the direction of the bungalow.

She turned and saw Allen running down the shore toward her. Ginny attempted to match his speed, but for once in her life, her runner's legs betrayed her and she dropped heavily to her knees. Every ounce of strength seemed to have abandoned her.

Then, an instant later, he was there. It was at that moment that she finally let down her guard. In the safety of Allen's arms, she cried until she could cry no more.

Weeks had passed since that awful night at Point Vedra Beach.

At first, Ginny had found it difficult to sleep through the night without waking in a blind panic. But, gradually, the sense of unease and the terrible memories seemed to fade and grew dimmer. By autumn, she was sleeping comfortably and awaking the following morning, feeling refreshed and in control once again.

Then, one night in October, she awoke to a burst of pain in the base of her skull. Her eyes opened wide, searching the darkness. A shadowy form hovered above her, holding a large syringe in one hand and a scalpel in the other. As a cloud passed and the moon sent its muted light through the bedroom window, she saw an orange jumpsuit and the gleam of broken manacles upon tanned wrists. And the familiar countenance of a face that was both dead and alive.

Wake up, Allen! her mind screamed, while her voice seemed strangely absent. *Please, wake up and help me!*

Her husband slept on the opposite side of the bed, completely oblivious to the danger she was in.

"It makes no difference to me, dear Ginny," whispered Jason Hargrove as he brought the half-moon blade of the scalpel downward. "Male or female, a donor is simply a donor to me."

Then she awoke with a start, nearly throwing the covers, along with Boo and Bogie, onto the floor. A strong, comforting hand reached out for her and her heartbeat settled.

"Are you alright, darling?" Allen asked her in the darkness.

Ginny said nothing. She simply cuddled against him, sure in the fact that she was rooted in blessed reality once again.

"Did you dream about *him?*"

"Just go back to sleep. I'm okay."

But she knew Allen didn't believe that. And, worst of all, she didn't believe it either.

After that night, she no longer trusted strangers as freely as she once had. She found herself avoiding those who wore prosthetic devices and felt her heart leap when the name Hargrove was mentioned.

And never again did she take moonlit walks during a midnight tide.

THE DARK TRIBE

"HEY, Josh… over here. I think I found something."

Josh Martin bumped his forehead on the dusty stud of the crawl-space ceiling for the third time that afternoon. He shook his head, trying to clear away the darting pinpricks of light, then joined his best friend at the far end of the four-foot cavity between bare earth and the reinforced floor of the Martin house.

They had gotten the idea of the excavation from a PBS special about dinosaurs the night before. Or, rather, it had been Andy Judson's idea. Josh had been reluctant about digging around for ancient dinosaur bones, especially since the proposed site was directly beneath his own house. But Andy always had that annoying way of talking him into things he really didn't want to do. And he usually ended up paying dearly for their little escapades, too, by getting grounded or receiving a sound whipping from his dad.

So far, they hadn't discovered a single dinosaur bone, not even a crummy fossil. He should have listened to his father, who was a professor of archaeology at nearby Duke University. He had told him that there was little chance of anyone finding dinosaur bones in that part of North Carolina. Josh had passed that information on to Andy, but his friend was thoroughly convinced that their native soil contained the petrified remains of lumbering Triceratops and Tyrannosaurus Rex… and that they had roamed the earth on which Josh's two-story house now stood.

Andy's sudden announcement of a discovery after three hours of digging gave Josh renewed hope. Maybe they weren't getting into trouble for nothing after all.

"What'd you find?" he asked. Then his breath caught in his throat as he peeked over his friend's shoulder and found himself staring into the face of a skull.

"Man, somebody's done gone and buried a body under your house," Andy said, his chubby face flush with excitement. "Have any of your old man's students turned up missing lately? Maybe some chesty co-ed he had the hots for?"

"Very funny," Josh said. "And keep your voice down, will you? If my mom hears us down here, she'll pitch a fit."

Andy reached down to grab the skull by the dirt-caked hollows of its eye sockets and wrench it from its ancient grave, but Josh stopped him. "No, that ain't the way to do it. This is an important historical find. We have to be professional, like real archaeologists. Here, let me show you."

He retrieved a garden trowel and some other things from where he had been digging at the far end of the crawlspace. The summer sunlight threw diamond patterns through the latticework of the front porch foundation as he set to work, mimicking the actions of the scientists they had seen on the dinosaur show. First, he cleared away the excess dirt, inch by inch, careful not to disturb the position of the exposed cranium. Then he meticulously brushed away particles of dust and earth with a small paintbrush he had procured from Dad's workbench in the garage.

Soon, the skull was completely uncovered. It was old… incredibly old. It was smooth and pitted. Oddly enough, it was not the ivory color that denuded bone normally was. Instead, it had a peculiar charcoal gray hue. The lower jaw was there too, and all the teeth were present and accounted for. In contrast to the color of the skull, they were dark and almost pearly black. The skull grinned ghoulishly up at the two ten-year-old boys, giving them the creeps.

They continued with their work; painstakingly careful not to do any damage. By the time evening had rolled around and Mom was calling out the back door for Josh to wash up for supper, they had an entire skeleton lying in an open grave before them. It was completely intact, not a single gray bone out of place or missing.

"Who do you think he was?" asked Andy.

Josh shrugged. "I don't know. An Indian, probably. Maybe an old Cherokee. Dad says there were a lot of them around these parts before they had to leave and walk something called the Trail of Tears."

"Looks like this guy missed out on the marathon."

They were about to leave the dank, earthy confines of the crawl-space, when the lingering rays of the setting sun washed through the latticework and glinted on something hidden deep inside the skeleton's collapsed ribcage. Upon further inspection, they found it to be an arrowhead wedged tightly in the vertebrae of the spinal column, between the shoulder blades.

It was no ordinary arrowhead... not like those Josh had seen made of sandstone or chiseled flint. No, this one seemed to almost be transparent and of a sparkling blue color. It looked as if it might be crafted from molten glass, or maybe even from some precious jewel, like a sapphire.

Andy, of course, had his hand out, ready to pluck it from the bone.

Josh caught his wrist in time. "Are you terminally dumb or something? I told you before, this is really important stuff we've found here. We shouldn't move anything... not until I get Dad to take a look at it."

"You're the one who's short on brain cells, pal," Andy told him. "You're not actually thinking of letting your old man take all the credit, are you? That's what he'll do, you know. He's a big-shot college professor, while we're only a couple of stupid kids. Figure it out for yourself."

Josh knew he was probably right. "What should we do then?"

"Let's stick with the digging for a couple of days. Maybe we can find more old bones, maybe some pottery or a neat tomahawk or two. Then we'll drag your dad into the limelight... but only after we make sure that we get most of the credit. Okay?"

"Okay," Josh agreed and they shook on it. Then Mom called for him again—a little crankier this time—and they scurried from beneath the house and went to their respective supper tables, covered from head to toe in dank soil and spider webs.

As the month of June came to an end and the Fourth of July approached, Josh and Andy continued their work in the crawlspace of the Martin house. In a span of two weeks, they had uncovered five more skeletons, bringing the final count to a grand total of six. All were ancient and amazingly intact, and all possessed the same puzzling gray color.

Also, all six possessed the same strange blue arrowheads wedged within their fleshless bodies. Some were caught between ribs, while others were stuck between the discs of spines or the tight crevices of leering skulls.

"Really weird about these arrowheads," Andy said for the umpteenth time. "Can't we just pry one of them out? It'd make a neat good luck charm, along with my rabbit foot and lucky buckeye."

Josh was unswayed on the professionalism of crawlspace archaeology, however. "Not yet. First, we'll get Dad and some of the other eggheads at the university to take a look at all this. Then maybe we can each have one of these arrowheads to keep."

Andy grumbled in agreement and, again, they left at the call of suppertime.

Later that night, after he had accompanied his folks to the grocery store in quest of wieners and chips for the big Fourth of July cookout the Martins were having the following evening, Josh caught his father alone in his study.

"Are there any Indian burial mounds around here?" he asked, trying to be as casual as possible.

"Sure," said Dad. "There must be hundreds of them around these parts. But they are all considered to be sacred ground, like a regular cemetery. In fact, it's against the law to dig up a mound. The Cherokee people worked long and hard to have their ancient grounds protected by federal law. Anyone can be sent to prison for desecrating the grave of a Native American."

Josh swallowed hard and said nothing.

The professor smiled and eyed his son, figuring maybe he was game for a good ghost story, now that they were on the subject of Indian history.

"You know, there was one tribe of Native Americans here in North Carolina that I don't think anyone would mind you digging up. In fact, we at the university have been trying to locate their particular burial ground for years, without success. They were called *Necropato* or "The Dark Tribe" by the other Indians who settled here in the Carolinas back before the white man showed up.

"According to Cherokee lore, the Dark Tribe was not even human, but a race of foul demons in Indian form. The Necropato were said to have been a savage tribe who raided neighboring villages, killing the Cherokee warriors in the most unspeakable ways and stealing their womenfolk to serve as unwilling brides. Every once in a while an abducted squaw would escape and return, white-haired and insane, to tell the Cherokee elders of the godless horrors the Necropato had inflicted upon them. They told of human sacrifice, cannibalism, and the horrid offspring they had been forced to bear for the evil warriors.

"Finally, the Cherokee medicine man prayed to the Great Spirit, who, in a dream, directed him to a large, blue stone in a creek. The shaman searched for the crystal stone for many days and eventually found it in the place of his dream. The Great Spirit told him that it possessed the power to vanquish certain evils from the face of the earth. He fashioned arrowheads from the blue stone and gave them to the bravest warriors of the tribe, who then headed into the dark forest of the Necropato to engage in battle. A great fight was said to have been waged between good and evil that night, and in the end, the Cherokee emerged victorious. The bodies of the cursed Necropato were buried in graves long forgotten, the cause of their destruction still lodged deep within their bodies; a precaution to ensure that their great evil would never rise to fight another day."

"Uh, that was... interesting, Dad," was all that Josh said before excusing himself.

The spooky tale had given him goosebumps. That night he laid awake in bed, afraid to go to sleep on the chance that he might dream of the Necropato and their savage atrocities. Finally, he got up and, taking a flashlight from the kitchen drawer, went outside into the humid July night. He stood outside the entrance of the crawlspace before he finally got up the nerve to squeeze inside.

He went from one skeleton to the next, flashing pale light upon their naked bones. Something about them seemed different, something he couldn't quite put his finger on. Maybe they just looked different in the darkness than they did in daylight.

On his way back out, he stopped beside the one nearest the crawlspace door and studied its grinning skull in the battery-powered glow. Yes, there was something different! The surface of the gray bones held no stain of age to them, as if the flesh of the long-dead warrior had rotted away only hours before, instead of hundreds of years ago. He laid his hand upon a lanky femur bone. His fingers recoiled in disgust. The bone was damp and oddly warm to the touch.

Probably just the humidity, he assured himself before heading back to the safety of his bedroom. But when he got there, he found no comfort. He lay awake half the night, certain that he could hear the sound of ragged breathing echo from the cracks of the floorboards beneath his bed.

The next day was full of fun and activity.

The Martin's backyard bustled with laughter and good spirits.

Little kids climbed on swing sets and the old timers pitched horse-shoes. Soon, afternoon darkened into evening. Dad set up the grill and began to cook up burgers and hotdogs, while Mom and some of the neighborhood ladies passed out paper plates, napkins, and plastic forks for the big meal. Later, there would be sparklers and fireworks to look forward to.

After they had eaten and watched fireworks, Josh and Andy decided to sneak into the crawlspace and check out their archaeological find. Night had already fallen and they knew it would be dark in the crawlspace, so Josh fetched the flashlight. When none of the grownups were looking, they squeezed through the little trap-door and stared across the raw earth that stretched beneath the foundation of the house.

In fact, that was all the two boys could do... stare in sudden, sinking confusion.

The skeletons were gone. Only the shadowy pits of their shallow graves remained.

"Cripes!" said Andy. "Where are they?"

Josh said nothing at first. A horrible thought crossed his mind, a thought that stretched the boundaries of what his youthful mind could normally comprehend. Then it hit him. He knew now what had been different about the skeletons last night... or rather, what had been *missing*. He turned to Andy, who crouched in puzzlement beside him, and fixed him with an accusing glare. Then he told him the story of the Necropato.

After he finished, he locked eyes with his best friend. "Did you do it?" he demanded of the pale and frightened boy. "Huh? You better fess up right now or I swear I'll pound you so hard..."

"Yes," confessed Andy. "I came back yesterday evening, after you went to supper."

Josh's eyes were grim. "Where are *they*?"

Andy fumbled through the pockets of his grass-stained jeans. His pudgy fist extended and opened. In the sweaty palm lay six crystal blue arrowheads.

Josh was about to launch himself at Andy in a fit of anger when something stopped him. Something outside. Something they could not see, but could hear quite clearly through the cinderblock foundation of the old house.

Screams lanced through the clear night air. There were two types of screaming. One was the shrill screaming reminiscent of old western movies; savage war cries that heralded the coming of torture and death to many an unfortunate wagon train. The other screaming was that typical of the horror movies he and Andy sometimes rented from the video store. The panicked shrieks of helpless victims as they fled from insectile aliens or chainsaw-slinging maniacs.

Then the screaming stopped and, in its place, came a much more hideous sound. The awful rending and tearing of human flesh, as well as the splatter and slow drip of warm, red blood saturating the summer clover and the dusty earth beneath the swings. And there was another, more distinctive noise; a great ripping and sucking sound, like strips of Velcro being slowly pulled apart.

Josh and Andy crouched there in the shadows. They listened… afraid to move, afraid to even breathe. Then they heard the soft padding of bare feet circling the house, coming ever closer. They sensed movement at the crawlspace door. Josh turned the flashlight toward the intruder and suddenly wished he had not, as a towering form loomed into view.

"Boy, is your old man gonna be PO'd!" said Andy.

Josh figured that he already was.

For as the dark warrior began to squeeze through the opening, long-bladed kitchen knife in hand, he smiled with familiar lips and stared at them from the ragged pits of stolen eyeholes.

And he was wearing Dad's skin.

TYROPHEX-14

JASPER HORNE KNEW something was wrong when he heard the cows screaming.

He was halfway through his breakfast of bacon, eggs, and scorched toast when he heard their agonized bellows coming from the north pasture. At first, he couldn't figure out what had happened. He had done his milking around five o'clock that morning and herded them into the open field at six. It was now only half past seven and his twelve Jersey heifers sounded as if they were simultaneously being skinned alive.

Jasper left his meal and, grabbing a twelve-gauge shotgun from behind the kitchen door, left the house. He checked the double-aught loads, then ran across the barnyard and climbed over the barbwire fence. It was a chilly October morning and a light fog clung low to the ground. Through the mist he could see the two-toned forms of the Jerseys next to the Clearwater stream that ran east-to-west on the Horne property. As he made his way across the brown grass and approached the creek bed, Jasper could see that only a few cows were still standing. Most were on their sides, howling like hoarse banshees, while others staggered about drunkenly.

Good God Almighty! thought Jasper. *What's happening here?*

A moment later, he reached the pasture stream. He watched in terror as his livestock stumbled around in a blind panic. Their eyes were wild with pain and their throats emitted thunderous cries, the likes of which Jasper Horne had never heard during sixty years of Tennessee farming.

The tableau that he witnessed that morning was hideous. One cow after

another dropped to the ground and was caught in the grip of a terrible seizure. Their tortured screams ended abruptly with an ugly sizzling noise and they lay upon the withered autumn grass, twitching and shuddering in a palsy of intense agony. Then the sizzling became widespread and the inner structures of the Jerseys seemed to collapse, as if their internal organs and skeletal systems were dissolving. A strange, yellowish vapor drifted from the bodily orifices of the milk cows, quickly mingling with the crisp morning air. Then the black and white skins of the heifers slowly folded inward with a hissing sigh, leaving flattened bags of cowhide lying limply along the shallow banks of the rural stream.

Numbly, Jasper approached the creek. He walked up to one of the dead cows and almost prodded it with the toe of his work boot, but thought better of it. He couldn't understand what had happened to his prime milking herd. They had been at the peak of health an hour and a half ago, but now they were all gone, having suffered some horrible mass death. Jasper thought of the stream and crouched next to the trickling current. He nearly had his fingertips in the water when he noticed the nasty yellow tint of it. And it had a peculiar smell to it too, like a combination of urine and formaldehyde.

The farmer withdrew his hand quickly, afraid to explore the stream any further. He stood up and puzzled over the dozen cow-shaped silhouettes that lay around the pasture spring. Then he headed back to the house to make a couple of phone calls.

· · ·

"I don't know what to tell you, Jasper," said Bud Fulton. "I can't make heads or tails of what happened here." The Bedloe County veterinarian knelt beside one of the dead animals and poked it with a branch from a nearby sour gum tree. The deflated hide unleashed a noxious fart, then settled even further until the loose skin — now entirely black and gummy in texture — was scarcely an inch in thickness.

"Whatever did it wasn't natural, that's for sure," said Jasper glumly.

The local sheriff, Sam Biggs, lifted his hat and scratched his balding head. "That goes without saying," he said, frowning at the closest victim, which resembled a cow-shaped pool of wet road tar more than anything else. "Do you think it could have been some kind of odd disease or something like that, Doc?"

"I don't believe so," said Bud. "The state agricultural bureau would have contacted me about something as deadly as this. No, I agree with Jasper. I think it must have been something in the stream. The cows must have ingested some sort of chemical that literally dissolved them from the inside out."

"Looks like it rotted away everything; muscle, tissue, and bone," said Jasper. "What could do something like that?"

"Some type of corrosive acid maybe," replied the vet. He squatted next to the stream and studied the yellowish color of the water for a moment. Then he stuck the tip of the sourgum branch into the creek. A wisp of bright yellow smoke drifted off the surface of the water and, when Bud withdrew the stick, the first four inches of it were gone.

"Well, I'll be damned!" said Sheriff Biggs. "That water just gobbled it right up, didn't it?" He took a wary step back from the stream.

Bud nodded absently and tossed the entire stick into the creek. They watched as it dissolved completely and the ashy dregs washed further downstream. "I'm going to take a sample of this with me," said the vet.

The doctor opened his medical bag and took out a small glass jar that he used for collecting urine and sperm samples from the area's livestock. He lowered the mouth of the container to the surface of the stream, but dropped it the moment the glass began to smolder and liquefy. "What the hell have we got here?" he wondered aloud as the vial melted and mingled with the jaundiced currents, becoming as free and flowing as the water itself.

The three exchanged uneasy glances. Jasper Horne reached into the side pocket of his overalls and withdrew a small engraved tin that he kept his smokeless tobacco in. He opened it, shook the snuff out of it, and handed it to the veterinarian. "Here, try this."

Bud Fulton stuck the edge of the circular container into the creek and, finding that the chemical had no effect on the metal, dipped a quantity of the tainted water out and closed the lid. He then took a roll of medical tape, wrapped it securely around the sides of the tobacco tin, and carefully placed it in his bag. "I'll need another water sample," he told Jasper. "From your well."

Jasper's eyes widened behind his spectacles. "Lordy Mercy! You mean to say that confounded stuff might've gotten into my water supply?" He paled at the thought of taking an innocent drink from the kitchen tap and ending up like one of his unfortunate heifers.

"Could be, if this chemical has seeped into an underground stream," said Bud. "I'm going to make a special trip to Nashville today and see what the boys at the state lab can come up with. If I were you, Jasper, I wouldn't use a drop of water from that well until I get the test results."

"I'll run into town later on and buy me some bottled water," agreed Jasper. "But where could this stuff have come from?" The elderly farmer wracked his brain for a moment, then looked toward the east with sudden suspicion in his eyes. "Sheriff, you don't think...?"

Sam Biggs had already come to the same conclusion. "The county landfill. This stream runs right by it."

"Dammit!" cussed Jasper. "I knew that it would come to something like this

when they voted to put that confounded dump near my place! I always feared that this creek would get polluted and poison my animals, and now it's done gone and happened!"

"Now, just calm down, Jasper," said the sheriff. "If you want, we can drive over to the landfill and talk to the fellow in charge. Maybe we can find out something. But you've got to promise to behave yourself and not go flying off the handle."

"I won't give you cause to worry," said Jasper, although anger still flared in his rheumy eyes. "Are you coming with us, Doc?"

"No, I think I'll go on and take these water samples to Nashville," said Bud. "I'm kind of anxious to find out what those state chemists have to say. I'm afraid there might be more at stake here than a few cows. The contamination could be more widespread than we know."

"What are you saying, Mr. Horne?" asked Alan Becket, the caretaker of the Bedloe County landfill. "That I deliberately let somebody dump chemical waste in this place?"

Jasper Horne jutted his jaw defiantly. "Well, *did* you? I've heard that some folks look the other way for a few bucks. Maybe you've got some customers from Nashville who grease your palm for dumping God-knows-what in one of those big ditches over yonder."

Sheriff Biggs laid a hand on the farmer's shoulder. "Now, you can't go making accusations before all the facts are known, Jasper. Alan has lived here in Bedloe County all his life. We've known him since he was knee-high to a grasshopper. That's why we gave him the job in the first place; because he can be trusted to do the right thing."

"But what about that stuff in my stream?" asked the old man. "If it didn't
come from here, then where the hell did it come from?"

"I don't know," admitted Sam Biggs. He turned to the caretaker. "Can you think of anything out of the ordinary that might've been dumped here, Alan? Maybe some drums with strange markings, or no markings at all?"

"No, sir," declared Becket. "I'm careful about what I let folks dump in here. I check everything when it comes through the gate. And if someone had come around wanting to get rid of some chemicals on the sly, I'd have called you on the spot, Sheriff."

Biggs nodded. "I figured as much, Alan, and I'm sorry I doubted you." The lawman stared off across the dusty hundred acre landfill. A couple of bulldozers could be seen in the distance, shoveling mounds of garbage into deep furrows. "You don't mind if we take a look around, do you? Just to satisfy our curiosity?"

"Go ahead if you want," said the caretaker. "I doubt if you'll find anything, though."

Sheriff Biggs and Jasper Horne took a leisurely stroll around the dusty expanse of the county landfill. They returned to the caretaker's shack a half hour later, having found nothing of interest. "I told you I run things legitimately around here, Sheriff," Alan said as he came out of the office.

"Still could be something out there," grumbled Jasper, not so convinced. "A man can't look underground, you know."

"We can't go blaming Alan for what happened to your cows," Biggs told the farmer. "That creek runs under the state highway at one point. Somebody from out of town might have dumped that chemical off the bridge. We can ride out and take a quick look."

"You can if you want," said Jasper. "I've pert near wasted half a day already. I've got some chores to do around the farm and then I've gotta run into town for some supplies." He cast a parting glance at the barren acreage of the landfill. Although he didn't mention it openly, Jasper could swear that the lay of the land was different somehow, that it had changed since the last time he had brought his garbage in. The land looked *wrong* somehow. It seemed *lower*, as if the earth has sunk in places.

Alan Becket accepted the sheriff's thanks for his cooperation, then watched as the two men climbed back into the Bedloe County patrol car and headed along the two-lane stretch of Highway 70.

After the car had vanished from sight, a worried look crossed the caretaker's face and he stared at the raw earth of the landfill. But where there was only confusion and suspicion in the farmer's aged eyes, an expression of dawning realization shown in the younger man's face. He watched the bulldozers work for a moment, then went inside his office. Alan sat behind his desk and, taking his wallet out of his hip pocket, fished a business card out of it.

The information on the card was simple and cryptic. There were only two lines of print. The first read TYROPHEX-14, while the second gave a single toll-free phone number.

Alan Becket stared at the card for a moment, then picked up the phone on his desk and dialed the number, not knowing exactly what he was going to say when he reached his contact on the other end of the line.

It was about six o'clock that evening when Jasper Horne left the county seat of Coleman and returned to his farm. After catching up on his chores that afternoon, Jasper had driven his rattletrap Ford pickup to town to pick up a few groceries and several gallon jugs of distilled water. He felt nervous and cagey during the drive home. He had stopped by the veterinary clinic, but Bud's wife — who was also his assistant — told him that the animal doctor hadn't returned from Nashville yet and hadn't called in any important news. He had checked with Sheriff Biggs too, but the constable assured him that he hadn't learned anything either. He had also told Jasper that he and his deputies had been unable to find any trace of illegal dumping near the highway bridge.

However, that didn't ease Jasper's mind any. He could picture himself forgetting the grisly events of that day, maybe stepping sleepily into the shower tomorrow morning and melting away beneath a yellowish cascade of deadly well water. He forced the disturbing image from his mind and drove on down the highway.

He was approaching the driveway of his property when he noticed that a South Central Bell van was parked smack-dab in the middle of the gravel turnoff. Jasper craned his neck and spotted a single repairman standing next to a telephone pole a few yards away, looking as though he had just shimmied down after working on the lines.

Jasper tooted his horn impatiently and glared through his bug-speckled windshield. The man lifted a friendly hand and nodded, walking around to the rear of the van to put his tools away. The old farmer drummed his fingers on the steering wheel and glanced in his rearview mirror to see if there were any vehicles behind him. There weren't. The rural road was deserted in both directions.

When Jasper turned his eyes back to the road ahead, he was startled to see that the telephone repairman was standing directly in front of his truck, no more than twelve feet away. The tall, dark-haired man with the gray coveralls and the sunglasses smiled humorlessly at him and lifted something into view. At first, Jasper was certain that the object was a jackhammer. It had the appearance and bulk of one. But on second glance, he knew that it was a much stranger contraption that the man held. It had the twin handles of a jackhammer, but the lower part of the tool resembled some over-sized gun more than anything else. There was a loading breech halfway down and, beneath that, a long barrel with a muzzle so large that a grown man could have stuck his fist inside it.

"What in tarnation...?" began Jasper. Then his question lapsed into shocked silence as the repairman aimed the massive barrel squarely at the truck and fired once.

Jasper ducked as the windshield imploded. The projectile smashed through the safety glass and lost its force upon entering the truck cab, bouncing off one of the padded cradles of the gun rack in the rear window. Jasper looked up just as the cylindrical object of titanium steel landed on the seat next to him. He stared at it for a moment, not knowing what to make of the repairman's attack or the thing he had fired into the truck. Then the old man's confusion turned into panic as the projectile popped into two halves and began to emit a billowing cloud of yellow smoke. He knew what it was the moment he smelled the cloying scent. It was the same rancid odor he had gotten a whiff of that morning at the creek.

Jasper Horne wanted to open the truck door and escape, but it was already too late. He was engulfed by the dense vapor, and was suddenly swallowed in a smothering cocoon of unbearable agony. That sizzling noise sounded in his ears, but this time it came from his own body. He felt his clothing fall away like blackened cinders and his skin begin to dissolve, followed by the stringy muscle and hard bone underneath. He recalled the screams of his Jersey cows and soon surpassed their howls of pain… at least until he no longer had a throat with which to vent his terror.

The following morning, Bud Fulton received an urgent call from Sheriff Biggs, wanting him to come to Jasper Horne's place as soon as possible.

Bud didn't expect to find what he did when he arrived. A county patrol car and a Lincoln sedan with federal plates were parked on the shoulder of the highway. Only a few yards from Jasper's driveway was a blackened hull that looked as if it might have once been a Ford pickup truck. It contained no glass in its windows and no tires on the rims of its wheels. A knot of cold dread sat heavily in the vet's stomach as he parked his jeep behind the police car and climbed out. Slowly, he walked over to where three men stood a safe distance from the body of the vehicle. One was Sam Biggs, while the other two were well-groomed strangers wearing tailored suits and tan raincoats.

The sheriff introduced them. "Bud, these gentlemen are Agents Richard Forsyth and Lou Deckard from the FBI." Forsyth was a heavy-set man in his mid-forties, while Deckard was a lean black man with round eyeglasses.

Bud shook hands with the two, then turned his eyes back to the truck. "What happened here?" he asked Biggs. "Damn, this is old Jasper's truck, isn't it? Did it burn up on him?"

"No," said Deckard. "The truck body hasn't been scorched. The black you see on the metal is oxidation. Something ravaged both the exterior and interior of this vehicle, but it wasn't fire. No, it was nothing as simple as that."

The veterinarian stared at the federal agent, then at the sheriff. "It was that damned chemical, wasn't it, Sam? But how did it get in Jasper's truck?" He peered through the glassless windows of the truck, but saw no sign of a body inside. "Where the hell is Jasper? Don't tell me he's..."

"I'm afraid so," replied the sheriff, looking pale and shaken. "Take a look inside, but be careful not to touch anything. Agent Deckard is a chemist, and he thinks the black residue on the truck might still be dangerous."

Cautiously, Bud stepped forward and peeked into the cab of the truck. Like the rubber of the tires and the glass of the headlights and windows, the vinyl of the dashboard and the cushions of the truck seat had strangely dissolved, leaving only oxidized metal. Amid the black coils of the naked springs lay a pile of gummy sludge that resembled the remains of the dead cows. In the center of the refuse were a number of shiny objects, all metal; a couple of gold teeth, a pocket watch, the buttons off a pair of Liberty overalls, and the steel frames of a pair of eyeglasses, minus the lenses.

Bud stumbled backward, knowing that the bits of tarnished metal were all that was left of his friend and fishing buddy, Jasper Horne.

"We appreciate you bringing this to our attention, Mr. Fulton," said Agent Forsyth. "I know you must have been frustrated yesterday when the state lab refused to give you the test results of the samples you brought in, but we thought it best to have Agent Deckard analyze them before we released any information to local law enforcement or civilians in the area. We had to be certain that they matched up with the other samples we have in our possession."

The veterinarian looked at the FBI agent. "Do you mean to tell me that this has happened before?"

"Yes," said Deckard. "Three times in the past six months. We've done our best to keep it under wraps and out of the news media. You see, this is a very delicate investigation we have going. And the chemical involved is a very dangerous and unpredictable substance."

"Do you know what it is?" Bud asked him.

"It is a very sophisticated and potent type of acid. More precisely, it is a super enzyme. From the tests we've ran on the previous samples, it is not biological in nature, but completely synthetic. It can digest almost anything; organic matter, paper, plastic, wood, and glass. The only thing that it has no destructive effect on is metal and stone. We believe it was produced under very strict and secretive conditions. In fact, its development might well have been federally funded."

"You mean the government might be responsible for this awful chemical?"

asked Bud incredulously.

Agent Forsyth looked a little uncomfortable. "We haven't been able to trace its origin as of yet. That's what Agent Decker and I are here to find out. You must understand, Mr. Fulton, the United States government funds thousands of medical, agricultural, and military projects every year. It is possible that one of these projects accidentally or intentionally developed this particular enzyme and that it somehow got into the wrong hands, or has been unscrupulously implemented by its manufacturer."

"Do you have any leads in the case?" asked the sheriff.

"We have several that are promising," said Deckard. "The previous incidents concerning this chemical took place in Nebraska, Texas, and Maryland. There seems to be only one solid connection between those incidents and the ones here in Tennessee."

"And what is that?"

"Municipal and rural landfills. There has always been one within a few miles of the reported incidents."

Sam Biggs and Bud Fulton exchanged knowing glances. "So old Jasper was on the right track after all," said the vet. "Do you think Alan Becket might have something to do with this?"

The sheriff shook his head. "I don't know. I was sure that Alan was a straight-shooter, but maybe he isn't as kosher as we thought."

"I suggest we pick up this Becket fellow for questioning," said

Forsyth. "He might just have the information necessary to wrap up this case."

The four climbed into their vehicles and headed east for the county landfill. None of them noticed that a van was following them at an inconspicuous distance. A telephone company van driven by a tall man wearing dark sunglasses.

It was seven o'clock that night when Alan Becket finally decided to come clean and tell them what they wanted to know.

Sam Biggs brought Becket from the cell he had been confined to for most of the day and led him to the sheriff's office on the ground floor of the Bedloe County courthouse. Alan took a seat, eyeing the men in the room with the nervous air of a caged animal. Agent Forsyth was perched on the corner of a desk, looking weary and impatient, while Agent Deckard and Bud Fulton leaned against a far wall. Despite his veterinary business, Bud had decided to stick around and see how the investigation turned out. Jasper Horne had been a close friend of Bud's and he wanted to see that justice was done, as far as the elderly farmer's death — or murder — was concerned.

"So, are you ready to level with us, Mr. Becket?" asked Forsyth.

"Yes, I am," said the man. "I've been thinking it over and I think it would be in my best interest to tell you everything. But, believe me, I had no idea that what I did was illegal or unethical. And I certainly didn't think that it would end up killing anyone."

"Why don't you tell it from the beginning," urged the FBI man. "And take your time."

With a scared look in his eyes, Alan Becket took a deep breath and began to talk. "It happened a couple of months ago. A man came to the landfill office. He claimed to be a salesman for a chemical firm called Tyrophex-14. At first, I thought it was a pretty peculiar name for a corporation, but after he made his sales pitch, it didn't seem so odd after all. He said that his company manufactured a chemical called Tyrophex-14, and that the chemical digested non-biodegradable waste… you know, like plastic and glass. It also sped up the decomposition process of paper, fabric, and wood. He said that one treatment per month in six calculated spots in the landfill would keep the volume of garbage to a minimal level. You see, after a month's worth of garbage was buried, a representative would arrive with a weird-looking contraption and inject this chemical, this Tyrophex-14, six feet into the earth. The capsule that held the chemical unleashed a gaseous cloud of the stuff, which wormed its way through the air pockets of the buried garbage and digested it.

"Let me tell you, it was a strange process. Minutes after the chemical was injected, the trash underneath seemed to simply disappear. The earth would sink, leaving empty ditches that were ready to be refilled and covered once again. In my eyes, it was a miraculous procedure and the cost was surprisingly affordable. I signed a one-year contract with the guy, sincerely thinking that I was doing it for the benefit of the community. I mean, just think of it. A perpetual landfill that digests its own garbage; a dumping ground that will never reach its projected capacity. I thought it was some sort of incredible environmental breakthrough, one that would do away with the need to find new landfill sites. The old ones could be used over and over again."

"But this miracle of modern science didn't turn out to be such a blessing after all, did it?" asked Forsyth. "At least not for Jasper Horne, and nine other human victims that we know of."

"I'm sorry," said Becket. "I know I should have checked it out, or at least okayed it with the county commissioner before I signed that contract. It was just that I didn't see any need to. The monthly treatments were only a few hundred dollars, and the county allots me twice that amount for supplies and maintenance."

"How do you get in touch with this corporation?" asked Forsyth. "Did they leave an address or name of the sales representative?"

"No, just a card with a phone number on it. It's in my wallet."

Agent Forsyth exchanged a triumphant glance with his partner Deckard, then turned to the county constable. "Sheriff, could you please get me Mr. Becket's wallet? I'll call the phone number into the bureau office in Nashville and have them trace it. It shouldn't be long before we know exactly who has been distributing this synthetic enzyme across the country."

Sheriff Biggs was about to open the side drawer of his desk and get Becket's personal property when the upper pane of the office's single window shattered. "Get down!" yelled Forsyth, drawing his gun and hugging the floor. The others followed suit – all except Alan Becket. The caretaker of the county landfill merely sat frozen in his chair as a cylindrical projectile of shiny steel spun through the hole in the window and landed squarely in his lap.

"Oh God, *no!*" he screamed, recognizing the capsule for what it was. He

grabbed it and was about to toss it away when the pod snapped in half, engulfing him in a dense cloud of corrosive gas.

"Everybody out!" called Sheriff Biggs. "This way!" The other three obeyed, crawling across the room in the general direction of the office door. They could hear the crash of broken glass as two more projectiles were shot through the window. When they reached the temporary safety of the outer hallway, they rose to their feet and looked back into the room. They watched in horror as the screaming, thrashing form of Alan Becket dissolved before their eyes, along with the wooden furnishings and paperwork of the sheriff's office.

Two hissing pops signaled the activation of the second and third projectiles. "Let's get out of here!" said Deckard.

By the time they reached the front door of the courthouse, they could hear the creaking and crackling of the wall supports dissolving away and collapsing beneath the weight of the upper floor. They glanced back only once before escaping to the open space of the town square, and the sight they witnessed was truly a horrifying one. A rolling cloud of the yellow gas was snaking its way

down the hallway, leaving a trail of structural damage in its wake.

"The one who shot that stuff through the window!" Bud suddenly said. "Where is he?"

He was answered by the brittle report of a gunshot. He and Sam Biggs turned to see Agents Forsyth and Deckard rushing to a dark form that lay beneath an oak tree. They joined the FBI men just as they were holstering their guns and cuffing the man's hands behind his back. The tall, dark-haired man in the gray coveralls had been hit once in the calf of his right leg. Next to him lay the injection tool that the late Alan Becket had described. No one went near the thing or picked it up, afraid that they might accidentally trigger another lethal dose of Tyrophex-14.

A moment later, a thunderous crash sounded behind them and they turned. The Bedloe County courthouse had completely collapsed, its lower supports chemically eradicated by the spreading cloud of vaporous enzyme. All that was left were bricks and blackened file cabinets.

"Well, we finally got the story," called the voice of Richard Forsyth. "And believe me, it turned out to be a lot worse than we first suspected."

Sam Biggs and Bud Fulton looked up from their coffee cups as the two FBI agents entered the lounge of the federal building. It was almost midnight and the pair had been at it for hours, interrogating the man who had been responsible for the deaths of Jasper Horne and Alan Becket. From the weary, but satisfied expressions on their faces, the county sheriff and the rural vet could tell that they had finally cracked the killer's shell and gotten the information they wanted.

Forsyth and Deckard got themselves some coffee and sat down at the table. "First of all, the suspect's name is Vincent Carvell," said Forsyth. "He's a white-collar hitman; a trouble-shooter that hires out to major corporations and takes care of their dirty business. And it seems that his latest client paid him generously to help keep Tyrophex-14 a big secret."

"Exactly who was his client?" asked Bud.

"A major corporation whose name you would instantly recognize. We would reveal it, but unfortunately we can't, due to security risks," said Forsyth apologetically. "You see, this corporation manufactures some very well-known products. In fact, it is responsible for thirty percent of this country's pharmaceutical and household goods. What the public doesn't know is that its research and development department also does some government work on the side. Mostly classified projects for the military." The older agent sipped his coffee and looked to Deckard, passing the ball to him.

"Although we can't give you specific details," continued Deckard, "we can give you the gist of what Tyrophex-14 is all about. This corporation was doing some work for the Defense Department. Their scientists were attempting to develop an enzymatic gas to be implemented by the armed forces. It was originally intended to be used for chemical warfare in the event that similar weapons were used against our own troops. But the Defense Department pulled the plug on the project when the corporation's scientists perfected a gas that dissolved any type of matter, organic or otherwise, with the exception of metal and stone. Tests showed that it was very unstable and difficult to control, so the project was quickly terminated and hushed up."

"But what the Defense Department didn't know," said Forsyth, "was that this corporation had already produced quite a large quantity of this destructive chemical, which had been labeled Tyrophex-14. They did a battery of tests, unbeknownst to the federal government, to see if it had any practical commercial use. And, obviously, they believed they had found it. Maybe their intentions were good at first. Maybe they actually believed that they had discovered a solution to the earth's garbage problem. But, ultimately, they failed to seek the proper approval and chose to market it covertly. That was when the unstable properties of Tyrophex-14 got out of control... and began to kill innocent people."

"And they hired this hit man to hush things up?" asked Sheriff

Biggs. "He killed Jasper Horne and Alan Becket, just to cover up this corporation's tracks?"

"Yes, and he would have killed us too, if we hadn't escaped from the courthouse. Carvell figured he could erase the threat of discovery if the investigators and the evidence vanished in a cloud of Tyrophex-14."

The thought of having come so close to death cast an uneasy silence over the four men. They thought of the blackened hull of Jasper's pickup truck and the rubble of the Bedloe County courthouse, and thanked God that they hadn't fallen victim to that corrosive monstrosity that had been conjured from the union of raw elements and complex chemical equations.

A couple of nights after the collapse of the country courthouse, Bud Fulton sat alone in his den, stretched out in his recliner and sipping on a beer. The room was dark and the nightly news was playing on the television, but he wasn't really paying very much attention to what transpired on the screen. Instead, he thought of the phone call he had received at the clinic that day. It had been Sheriff Biggs, filling him in on the results of the FBI's midnight raid on the shadowy corporation responsible for manufacturing the deadly chemical gas known as Tyrophex-14.

Sam had told him that the raid had taken place discreetly and that it would remain a secret matter, solely between the federal government and their unscrupulous employee. The FBI had failed to say what sort of steps would be taken to see that the project was buried and that experimentation in that particular area was never explored again. But Agent Forsyth had volunteered one last bit of information, albeit disturbing, to repay Biggs and Fulton for keeping silent on the delicate matter.

Forsyth had said that the records of the corporation had listed twenty 50,000 gallon tanks as being the extent of the chemical's manufactured volume. But when the federal agents had checked the actual inventory, only seventeen of the tanks had been found on the company grounds.

Bud drove the sordid business from his mind and tried to concentrate on the work he had to do tomorrow. He was scheduled to give a few rabies and distemper shots in the morning, after which he would head to the Pittman farm to dehorn a couple of bad tempered bulls. Somehow, the simple practices of rural veterinary seemed downright tame compared to what he had been through the night before last.

Bud finished his beer while watching the local weather and sportscast. He was reaching for the remote control, intending to turn off the set and go to bed, when a news anchor appeared on the screen again with a special bulletin. Bud leaned forward and watched as the picture cut away to a live report.

A female reporter stood next to a train that had derailed a few miles north of Memphis, Tennessee. Firemen milled behind her and the wreckage was illuminated by the spinning blue and red lights of the emergency vehicles that had been called to the scene. The reporter was talking, informing the viewers of the details of the train derailment. But Bud Fulton's attention wasn't on the woman or the story that she reported.

Instead, his eyes shifted to the huge tanker car that lay overturned directly behind her. He prayed that he was mistaken, but his doubts faded when the TV camera moved in closer, bringing the details of the cylindrical car into focus.

Bud's heart began to pound as he noticed a wisp of yellow vapor drift, almost unnoticed, from a rip in one of the tanker's riveted seams. And, on the side of the ruptured car, were stenciled a series of simple letters and numbers. To those on the scene, and in the city beyond, they meant absolutely nothing. But to Bud Fulton, they were like the bold signature of Death itself.

And its name that night was Tyrophex-14.

THE BOXCAR

"HELLO THE CAMP!" I yelled down into that dark, backwoods hollow beside the railroad tracks. We could see the faint glow of a campfire and shadowy structures of a few tin and tarpaper shacks, but no one answered. Only the chirping of crickets and the mournful wail of a southbound train on its way to Memphis echoed through the chill autumn night.

"Maybe there ain't nobody down there," said Mickey. His stomach growled ferociously and mine sang in grumbling harmony. Me and Mickey had been riding the rails together since the beginning of this Great Depression and, although there were a number of years between us — he being a lad of fifteen years and I on into my forties — we had become the best of traveling buddies.

"Well, I reckon there's only one way to find out," I replied. "Let's go down and have a look-see for ourselves."

We slung our bindles over our shoulders and descended the steep grade to the woods below. We were bone-tired and hungry, having made the long haul from Louisville to Nashville without benefit of a free ride. It was about midnight when we happened across that hobo camp. We were hoping to sack out beside a warm fire, perhaps trade some items from our few personal possessions for coffee and a plate of beans.

As we skirted a choking thicket of blackberry bramble and honeysuckle, we found that the camp was indeed occupied. Half a dozen men, most as rail-thin and down on their luck as we were, sat around a crackling fire. A couple were engaged in idle conversation, while others whittled silently, feeding the flames of the campfire with their wood shavings. They all stopped stone-still when we emerged from the briar patch and approached them.

"Howdy," I said to them. "We called down for an invite, but maybe ya'll didn't hear."

A big, bearded fellow in a battered felt fedora eyed us suspiciously. "Yeah, we heard you well enough."

I stepped forward and offered a friendly smile. "Well, me and my partner here, we were wondering if we might... "

My appeal for food and shelter was interrupted when a scrubby fellow who had been whittling stood up, his eyes mean and dangerous. "Now you two just stay right where you are." I looked down and saw that he held a length of wooden tent stake in his hand. The end had been whittled down to a wickedly sharp point.

"We're not aiming to bother nobody, mister," Mickey spoke up. "We're just looking for a little nourishment, that's all."

One of the bums at the fire expelled a harsh peal of laughter. "Sure... I bet you are."

"Go on and get outta here, the both of you," growled the fellow with the pointy stick. He made a threatening move toward us, driving us back in the direction of the thicket. "Get on down the tracks to where you belong."

"We're a-going," I told them, more than a little peeved by their lack of hospitality. "A damn shame, though, folks treating their own kind in such a sorry manner, what with times as hard as they are these days."

Some of the men at the fire hung their heads in shame, while the others only stared at us with that same look of hard suspicion. "Please... just move on," said the big fellow.

Me and Mickey made the grade in silence and continued on down the tracks. "To heck with their stupid old camp," the boy said after a while. "Didn't wanna stay there anyhow. The whole place stank to the high heavens."

Thinking back, I knew he was right. There had been a rather pungent smell about that hobo camp. It was a thick, cloying odor, familiar, yet unidentifiable at the time. And, although I didn't mention it to Mickey, I knew that the hoboes' indifferent attitude toward us hadn't been out of pure meanness, but out of downright fear. It was almost as if they'd been expecting someone else to come visiting. Our sudden appearance had set them on edge, prompting the harsh words and unfriendliness that had let us know we were far from welcome there.

We moved on, the full moon overhead paving our way with nocturnal light. The next freight yard was some twenty or thirty miles away with nothing but woods and thicket in between. So it was a stroke of luck that we turned a bend in the tracks and discovered our shelter for the night.

It was an old, abandoned boxcar. The wheels had been removed for salvage and the long, wooden hull parked off to the side near a grove of spruce and pine. We waded through knee-high weeds to the dark structure. It was weathered by sun and rain. The only paint that remained was the faint logo of a long-extinct railroad company upon the side walls.

"Well, what do you think?" I asked young Mickey.

The freckle-faced boy wrinkled his nose and shrugged. "I reckon it'll have to do for tonight."

We had some trouble pushing the door back on its tracks, but soon we stepped inside, batting cobwebs from our path. The first thing that struck us was the peculiar feeling of soft earth beneath our feet, rather than the customary hardwood boards. The rich scent of freshly turned soil hung heavily in the boxcar, like prime farmland after a drenching downpour.

We found us a spot in a far corner and settled there for the night. I lit a candle stub so as to cast a pale light upon our meager supper.

It wasn't much for two hungry travelers; just a little beef jerky I had stashed in my pack, along with a swallow or two of stale water from Mickey's canteen. After we'd eaten, silence engulfed us — an awkward silence — and I felt the boy's concerned gaze on my face.

Finally, I could ignore it no longer. "Why in tarnation are you gawking at me, boy?"

Mickey lowered his eyes in embarrassment. "I don't know, Frank... you just seem so pale and peeked lately. And you get plumb tuckered out after just a couple hours walking. How are you feeling these days? Are you sick?"

"Don't you go worrying your head over me, young fella. I'm doing just fine." I lied convincingly, but the boy was observant. The truth was, I *had* been feeling rather poorly the last few weeks, tiring out at the least physical exertion and possessing half the appetite I normally had. I kept telling myself I was just getting old, but secretly knew it must be something more.

Our conversation died down and we were gradually lulled to sleep by the sound of crickets and toads in the forest beyond.

That night, I had the strangest chain of dreams I'd ever had in my life.

I dreamt that I awoke the following day to find Mickey and myself trapped inside the old boxcar. It was morning; we could tell by the warmth of the sun against the walls and the singing of birds outside.

We started in the general direction of the sliding door, but it was pitch dark inside, sunlight finding nary a crack or crevice in the car's sturdy boarding. We stumbled once or twice upon obstructions that hadn't been there the night before and finally reached the door. I struggled with it, but it simply wouldn't budge. It seemed to be fused shut. I called to Mickey to lend me a hand, but for some reason he merely laughed at me. Eventually, I tired myself out and gave up.

We returned to our bindles, again having to step and climb over things littering the floor. I lit a candle. The flickering wick revealed what we had been traipsing over in the darkness. There had to be twelve bodies lying around the earthen floor of that boxcar. The pale and bloodless bodies of a dozen corpses.

I grew frightened and near panic, but Mickey calmed me down. "They're only sleeping," he assured me with a toothy grin that seemed almost ominous.

Somehow, his simple words comforted me. Utterly exhausted, I lay back down and fell asleep.

The next dream began with another awakening. It was night this time and the boxcar door was wide open. The cool October breeze blew in to rouse me. I found myself surrounded by those who had lain dead only hours before. They were all derelicts and hoboes, mostly men, but some were women and children. They stared at me wildly, their eyes burning feverishly, as if they were in the heated throes of some diseased delirium. There seemed to be an expression akin to wanton hunger in those hollow-eyed stares, but also something else. Restraint. That kept them in check, like pale statues clad in second-hand rags.

I noticed that my young pal, Mickey, stood among them. The boy looked strangely similar to the others now. His once robust complexion had been replaced with a waxy pallor, like melted tallow. "You must help us, Frank," he said. "You must do something that is not in our power... something only *you* can perform."

I wanted to protest and demand to know exactly what the hell was going on, but I could only stand there and listen to what they had to say. After my instructions had been made clear, I simply nodded my head in agreement, no questions asked.

The dream shifted again.

It was still night and I was standing in the thicket on the edge of that hobo camp in the hollow. Carefully, and without noise, I crept among the make-shift shanties, performing the task that had been commanded of me. I removed the crude crosses, the cloves of garlic that hung draped above the doorways, and toted away the buckets of creek water that had been blessed by a traveling preacher man.

I spirited away all those things, clearing the camp, leaving only sleeping men. They continued their snoring and their unsuspecting slumber, totally oblivious to the danger that now descended from the tracks above.

I stood there in the thicket and listened as the horrified screams reached their gruesome climax, then dwindled. They were replaced by awful slurping and sucking sounds. The pungent scent of raw garlic had moved southward on the breeze. In its place hung another... a nasty odor like that of hot copper.

"Much obliged for the help," called Mickey from the door of a shanty, his eyes as bright as a cat's, lips glistening crimson. Then, with a wink, he disappeared back into the shack. The hellish sounds continued as I curled up in the midst of that dense thicket and, once again, fell asleep.

That marked the end of that disturbing chain of nightmares, for a swift kick in the ribs heralded my true awakening. It was broad daylight when I opened my eyes and stared up at an overweight county sheriff.

"Wake up, buddy," he said gruffly. "Time to get up and move on."

I stretched and yawned. Much to my amazement, I found myself not in the old boxcar, but in the camp side thicket. My bindle lay on the ground beside me. Confused, I rose to my feet and stared at the ramshackle huts and their ragged canvas overhangs. They looked to be completely deserted, as if no one had ever lived there at all.

"There were others..." I said as I tucked my pack beneath my arm.

The lawman nodded. "Someone reported a bunch of tramps down here, but it looks like they've all headed down the tracks. I suggest you do the same, if you don't want to spend the next ninety days in the county workhouse."

I took that sheriff's advice and, bewildered, started on my way.

After a quarter mile hike down the railroad tracks, I came to the boxcar.

"Mickey!" I called several times, but received no answer. Had the boy moved on, leaving me behind? It was hard to figure, since we'd been traveling the country together for so very long.

I tugged at the door of that abandoned boxcar, but I was unable to open it. I placed my ear to the door and heard nothing.

Since that night, much has taken place.

I've moved on down to Louisiana and back again, hopping freights when they're going my way and when the yard bulls aren't around to catch me in the act. Still, Mickey's puzzling departure continues to bug me. That grisly string of dreams preys on my mind as well. Sometimes it's mighty hard to convince myself that they actually *were* dreams.

Oh, and I found out why I've been so pale and listless lately. A few weeks ago, I visited my brother in Birmingham. Unlike me, he is a family man who made it through hard times rather well. He suggested I go see a doctor friend of his, which I did. The sawbones' verdict was halfway what I expected it to be.

For, you see, I'm dying. Seems that I have some sort of blood disease, something called leukemia. Now ain't that a bitch?

My dear brother insisted that I check into a hospital, but I declined. I've decided to spend my last days riding the rails. Who knows where I'll end up... perhaps lying face down in a dusty ditch somewhere or in a busy train yard, trying to jump my last freight.

However it turns out, I don't really mind. When my end does come, at least I'll have the satisfaction of knowing that mine will be a *real* death, deep and everlasting... and not one that is measured by the rising and the setting of the sun.

DUST DEVILS

THE BRUISES WERE NOT SO MUCH painful as they were downright ugly. Stan had put them there when he discovered the green and gold cheerleader uniform hanging from the knob of her closet door.

"What do you wanna be? A slut or something" her stepfather had bellowed in one of his drunken rages, which had seemed to grow in frequency since the death of her mother.

"Do you want them boys looking up your skirt whenever you do those somersaults and splits? Do you, huh? Cause you're a filthy, little tramp if you do. That's all cheerleaders are, anyway, you know. Just slutty teases, wagging their pretty asses in your face, getting a man all worked up for nothing!"

She had opened her mouth to object and he had lit into her like a wildcat. Before she had made it to the safety of her bedroom, he had put a half dozen good-sized bruises on her arms and legs and given her one hell of a black eye. She had awakened that Tuesday morning hoping, praying, that it wouldn't look as bad as she suspected it would... but, of course, it did. She had stayed home from school that day, from the try-outs she had looked forward to for nearly three weeks. Tomorrow the swelling would be down, reduced to an ugly yellow-brown patch around her left eye, and she would sadly return the cheerleader outfit to Mrs. Petty, the girls' cheerleading coach. She knew when she did, she would receive that awful look of pity; a look she had grown to hate like a poison.

Becky Mae Jessup spent the day in her cramped room at the rear of the house trailer. She lay in bed, watching the soaps on her black and white portable. A beautiful socialite was on the screen, downing martinis and valium, crying her eyes out because her executive husband was across town bedding his boss's wife.

"What do you know about being lonely?" she spat at the actress. "*Truly* lonely?" The thought almost angered her to tears. Loneliness was a sixteen-year-old girl in west El Paso whose heart soared whenever a boy — *any* boy — smiled her way or just said "Hi". Loneliness was crying yourself to sleep, thinking of the pretty clothes you would never own and the exotic places you could never hope to see.

She glanced over at her open closet door at the poster that hung inside; a poster of one of the hottest pop singers around. He smiled at her with those perfect, white teeth and she smiled back with teeth that were not so perfect or so white. Stan didn't know that she had it. If he had, he would have pitched a fit. "You ain't old enough to be thinking of such things," he constantly told her. "Next thing I know, you'll be knocked-up or have one of them damned venereal diseases!"

She always ignored his senseless ravings, though, seeing past his grumbling guidance to the hypocrisy underneath. For a man who seemed so all-fired concern with his stepdaughter's moral upbringing. Stan Jessup had no qualms whatsoever about the raunchy centerfolds that papered the walls of his own room, or the women he sometimes brought home from the Diamondback Saloon. *Loose women,* her mother used to call them with dismay, *common whores.* Some nights Becky Mae had to bury her head in her pillow to drown out the sounds of dirty laughter and the jouncing of bedsprings.

She grew weary of the endless scandals of daytime TV and went outside, stopping by the fridge for a soda. Becky Mae sat there on the rickety wooden steps of the weathered trailer, staring at the drab surroundings she had known for six years. Her mother had married Stan Jessup in '83, a few years after her real father had died in an oil rig explosion. Stan hadn't seemed like such a bad fellow until her mother died of lung cancer in the spring of '85. Then he had ruled over her with an iron fist, and that fist hurt, both physically and mentally.

The trailer park on the far reaches of the West Texas highway was owned by Connie Ketchum, a bird-like woman with brilliant red hair. She lived in the little adobe bungalow that doubled as the main office with her seven-year-old son, Tony. Mrs. Ketchum had run the park alone since her husband went out for a pack of Camels one morning and never came back. That had been five years ago.

Mrs. Ketchum was pruning the cactus around her patio when an unpleasant memory came to Becky Mae. She had been twelve then, right after her mother had come home from the hospital that last time. Mrs. Ketchum's face had been deadly serious. "Becky Mae," she had said, "does your stepdaddy ever touch you... in a *wrong way?*" Becky Mae hadn't known what she was referring to and told her so. The woman's face had blushed as red as her firebrand hair. "Never mind, dear," she had muttered, dismissing it as quickly as she had brought it up. "Just forget I ever mentioned it."

But she couldn't forget. And now, four years later, she knew exactly what Mrs. Ketchum had been getting at. Becky Mae had become slowly aware of Stan's growing attention toward her in the past few months. A couple of nights ago, he had reached across the table for the salt shaker and deliberately brushed her breast, chuckling at her sudden embarrassment. She was also aware of how his eyes followed her around the trailer when she wore a halter top and cutoffs in the summer.

A low whistling roused her from her place on the steps, and she walked around back. At first she could see nothing but the back lot, littered with trash and the rusty junkers her stepdad tinkered with on his time off. There was the railroad tracks and beyond that, the distant expanse of scrubby Mexican desert. The landscape appeared as desolate and lonely as she felt at the moment. The tears threatened to come then, but held off when the whistling sound grew louder, closer.

She could see it now, floating in from the west. A little whirlwind, a mini-twister, a *dust devil,* as her mother called them. What was it her bedridden mother had warned her about dust devils? *Don't you ever go near one, girl,* she had said, cigarette jutting from between lips swollen by chemotherapy. *And for God's sake, don't ever walk into the middle of one! Take it from me, they'll take ahold of you and tear your soul right out. It's true! I read it in the National Enquirer.*

She had never believed her, but now, watching the dusty funnel drift lazily toward her, bouncing over the steel rails and cross-ties into the backyard, Becky Mae almost could. She set her soda on the seat of a busted lawn chair and found herself walking directly into its weaving path.

The tears were flowing freely now. *Well, let's just see if it is true then,* she thought. *If it is, I don't care. Let it take my soul. Maybe I'll end up in a better place than the one I'm in right now.*

Slowly, erratically, the dust devil skimmed across the earth, drawing small pebbles and surface dust into its centrifuge. A mesquite branch snapped off its bush, caught up in the swirling packet of air, then discarded. Becky Mae continued forward. Ten feet stretched between them, then only five. Before she could give her actions a second thought, she closed her eyes and stepped into the center of the sand spout.

Surprisingly enough, there was no great force that tore at her, no turbulent howling within. Only a strange calm, as the eye of a hurricane might be. She kept her eyes screwed tightly shut so as not to get dust in them and simply stood there. The twister did not move beyond her, but stood stationary, cradling her within its hollow.

Abruptly, a strong feeling gripped the teenager. It was as if – yes, there was a *presence* of some sort there with her… inside the heart of the dust devil. A very lonely presence, one that ached for companionship. A decidedly *male* presence.

You're just imagining things, she told herself. But, on second thought, she didn't think so. The air currents swirled tenderly around her and, as she relaxed and let her troubles vanish, she strangely felt as though her clothing had suddenly slipped away. Tiny breezes like gentle hands caressed her bare skin, running masterfully along her small breasts, the flat of her stomach, the flare of her hips. An electric thrill traveled through her, from the base of her spine to the top of her head. *Is this how it feels to make love?* she wondered.

Then there was a pressure on her lips; a soft meshing of warm air against flesh... a spectral kiss from whatever haunted the spiral of dust. *Becky Mae,* a voice said, as if coming from some great distance.

"Yes," she gasped. "That's my name... what's yours?"

Silence. Then the voice came again, but different this time. Distinctly familiar and edged in anger. *Becky Mae... where the hell are you, girl?*

Startled, she backed out of the center of the little whirlwind, tripping and landing hard on her backside on the barren earth. The dust devil hovered there for a moment longer, then retreated back in the direction from which it came.

Stan, dressed in greasy coveralls and toting a lunch box, rounded the corner of the trailer and glared at his stepdaughter hatefully. "What in tarnation are doing down there?"

Becky Mae felt panic grip her, but when she looked down, she found her clothing to be intact. "Nothing. Just sitting here."

"Well, you ain't gonna have no ass left to sit on if you don't get up right quick," Stan warned. "Now, get on in the kitchen and put some supper on the table before I give you an instant replay of last night."

She did as he said. Before following him up the steps, she cast her eyes back across the broken horizon with its endless miles of buttes and sagebrush. *Nothing but an old dust devil, that's all,* she thought in disappointment. *Just a daydream.* But, somehow, she could not convince herself that what had happened that afternoon had been a trick of the mind, rather than something intimate and true.

Becky Mae's one and only boyfriend had been Todd Lewis, but their relationship had been short-lived, spanning all of thirty seconds. The senior had showed up at the trailer to take her to the double-feature at the Skyline Drive-In, but Stan had chased him off with a shotgun. Her stepfather had blown out the taillights of the boy's Mustang before he could make the safety of the main highway. Since that incident, no guy in his right mind came near Becky Mae Jessup, no matter how cute she was.

Now she awaited a boyfriend of a different kind, one that she could only hear in her mind, that she could only feel in the currents of the wind. She awaited him that Friday evening as she had for the past two days, sitting on the hood of an old Plymouth Duster in the backyard. For two days she had watched the dusty desert along the Texas-Mexico border for a fleeting sign of the dust devil. Each evening after school, she had stared across the sunbaked wilderness until darkness descended, leaving her depressed and disappointed once again.

This evening a new emotion joined the others. Fear sat heavy in her heart, not over the absence of the sand spout, but because of her stepfather. Mrs. Ketchum's cryptic words of four years ago came back to haunt her and she had a dreadful feeling that tonight would be the night that Stan would make his lurid move. Tonight he would finally try to touch her in that *wrong way*, or perhaps attempt something much worse.

She knew that it was so, the way he had acted over breakfast that morning, the way he had looked her square in the eyes over French toast and coffee. It was nearly six o'clock now. He had already clocked out from the garage and was on his way home. After supper, he would have a few shots of Wild Turkey to gather his nerve and then force his filthy self upon her. The thought of him close to her made her cringe in revulsion. Stan was a wiry man, but strong, and she was afraid that whatever he had in mind that night would take place, no matter how violently she struggled.

Tears threatened to come, but she fought them back. She didn't want her spectral lover to see her bawling like a baby. *You really are warped, you know that?* she scolded herself. *What happened the other day was just make believe, just a fantasy.* But no matter how many times she told herself that, she still could not escape the feeling that the lone dust devil was exactly what she thought it was; a wandering ghost, a kindred spirit as hungry for love and companionship as she was.

The setting sun hurt Becky Mae's eyes as she continued to survey the brilliant hues of the darkening horizon. A western breeze blew through her strawberry blond hair, a kiss blown from a thousand miles away. She closed her eyes and tried to imagine the sensation of gentle hands upon her body, delivering thrills of delight. Then a harsh voice from behind her dispersed the calm, filling her with an icy dread like a heavy stone in the pit of her gut.

"Are you out here *again*, girl?" Stan asked incredulously from the rear door of the trailer. "I swear I'm beginning to think you're retarded, Becky Mae. Now you get on in here and fix me some supper. You hear me?"

Becky Mae said nothing. She just sat there and stared across the deepening desert, praying... praying for a miracle and knowing very well that miracles did not happen in Ketchum's Trailer Park on the outskirts of El Paso, Texas.

"Dammit, girl, don't make me come out there and get you!"

Again, she ignored him and continued to wish for the impossible. *Please! Please come and take me away from this awful place. Come and sweep me away on the wings of the wind, away from El Paso, away from Texas, away from this world if you can.* She listened for the familiar whistle of the sand spout's approach, but heard nothing... nothing but Stan's angry footsteps crunching across the backyard, straight for her.

"You little smart-ass bitch!" growled Stan, grabbing her roughly by the arm. "You answer your elders when spoken to, understand? Now get your sassy butt inside that trailer before…"

She startled him by turning and giving him the dirtiest, most mean-eyed look she could muster. "Let go of me, Stan," she said, "or so help me I'll yell 'rape' to the high heavens."

Her stepfather was a little taken aback by her boldness, but not enough to relinquish his bruising hold. He stared at her for a long moment and a broad grin split his five o'clock shadow. "You know, don't you? You've known of my intentions all along. Well, you oughta know me well enough to know that there's no way out of it. You know I always get what I want, no two ways about it. And, by God, I'll have what I've set out to get tonight!" He pulled her bodily off the hood of the Plymouth and began to drag her toward the open trailer door.

Knowing that she had no other choice, Becky Mae screamed just as loud and with as much force as she possibly could.

"Shut up, you hear me?" said Stan. "Shut the hell up!" He loosened his hold long enough to give her a couple of backhand slaps across the face. She continued her screaming as she dropped to the ground and curled up to ward off the raining blows of his work-hardened fists. Her nose bled freely and her eyes began to swell shut as Stan's calloused knuckles fell time and time again.

"You can make it hard or you can make it easy," he warned, pulling a heavy leather belt from the loops of his trousers. "It's up to you. Shut your trap and crawl into that trailer and maybe I won't mess you up too bad tonight. But if you keep up that hollering, you might not make it to morning alive." When she continued her loud rebellion, Stan shook his head and, with a grin, raised the belt for the first downward stroke.

Then a howling from the west echoed over the desert like the roar of an impending doom.

"What in Sam Hill?" asked Sam in puzzlement. Becky Mae brought her head from beneath her crossed arms and, with battered, tearful eyes, stared toward the broken horizon. An imposing wall of dust the shade of burnt umber boiled toward them with a violent turbulence that obscured entire buttes and swept through the shallows of dry washes like an earthen tide.

Stan discarded his belt and, grabbing Becky Mae's arm and a fistful of her hair, began to back toward the trailer door. "Hell of a dust storm coming up, sweetheart," he snickered. "We'd better get on inside. Don't worry, though. We'll find something to keep ourselves occupied while we weather the storm."

Angrily, she batted ineffectively at him with her clenched fists, bringing howls of laughter rather than grunts of pain. They were almost ten feet from the open door when something totally unexpected happened. Unexpected for Stan perhaps, but not for Becky Mae. She had been hoping fervently for something to take place, something that would deliver her from the horrible fate Stan had in store for her.

The dust at the foot of the back steps began to boil. It rose skyward on spiraling currents of air until a dust devil seven feet high blocked Stan's pathway. It's color was not the soft beige that Becky Mae remembered from before, but an angry red. The twister bobbed and weaved like a boxer awaiting its opponent. Stan took a couple of steps to the side to go around it, but it shifted swiftly, stopping his progress. Then a fetid wind, like the winds of hell itself, washed over the man and his captive, roaring, demanding in bellowing currents of air... *Let her go!*

Stan stood there and gaped, wondering if he actually heard what he thought he had. Then he knew for certain when the dust devil barreled forward with a vengeance, firing grit with such force that it lodged in the pores of his skin. *I said... LET...HER...GO!*

The mechanic's natural bravado got the best of him. "The hell you say!" he growled, swaggering forward with Becky Mae in tow.

Before he knew it, it was upon him. A pain lanced through his wrist, as if every bone there had been shattered. Becky Mae escaped his grasp. She tumbled to the side and crouched against the gathering fury of the sandstorm. Stan, like the fool he was, swung blindly at the thing that had hold of him, but his blows flailed through the open air, hitting nothing. He moaned in terror as the dust devil lifted him within its swirling cone, the tiny rocks and cactus needles in the currents ripping at his clothing and flesh, drawing blood. He spun end over end, screaming madly as the wraith manhandled him, twisting and battering him until his entire body was racked with agony.

Then, when he thought he would surely be torn asunder, he was discarded like a rag doll. He was expelled from the cyclone with such force that he sailed through the open door of the trailer, across the cramped kitchenette, and landed headfirst into the cedarwood cabinet. He was out cold the second his skull split the hardened wood and bent the steel piping of the sink beyond.

Becky Mae lay trembling for a long moment and, when she thought it safe enough to lift her head, discovered that the dust storm had passed. Only the hovering dust devil, now its regular size and color, waited nearby. Her victorious suitor, her knight in shiny armor, so to speak.

She approached it with a smile on her blood-streaked face, her hands fidgeting nervously. "Thank you," she sobbed happily. "Oh, thank you so very much." She giggled as soft currents caressed her face, brushing away her tears. Then Stan came back to mind and she looked toward the open doorway of the trailer. He lay slumped across the peeling linoleum floor, pretty roughed up, but still alive. That meant that she had not yet escaped.

He would wake up eventually and, madder than before, insist on having his way with her. She would never be able to escape the lustful fury of Stan Jessup.

That was *unless…*

She started forward. In turn, the dust devil approached her in its smooth, shimmying gait. They stood there for a hesitant moment, regarding each other like two long-lost lovers. Then, closing her eyes, Becky Mae stepped into the heart of the funnel and let herself go.

. . .

Stan came to an hour later and found three men standing over him. One was a uniformed police officer, while the other two were plain-clothes detectives.

"Are you Stanley Jessup?" one asked him.

"Yeah. Who the hell are you?"

"El Paso Police Department, Mr. Jessup," they said, flashing their credentials. "Will you accompany us outside, please?"

With some effort, Stan picked himself up from the floor. He was a real mess. His clothes were torn and his face and arms were lacerated and scratched. "She sure put a hell of a fight, even if it didn't do her any good," the uniformed cop noted with some satisfaction. Stan couldn't figure out what he was driving at, until he reached the open door of the battered house trailer.

Several people stood in the backyard. There was Mrs. Ketchum and her son, two fire department paramedics, and, lying sprawled and misshapened on the sandy earth, was Becky Mae. His stepdaughter's clothes were nearly torn away, her slender limbs cocked at odd angles from her body. Her face was a mask of contradiction, wearing an expression torn between intense agony and blissful rapture. A light powdering of dust coated the orbs of her open eyes.

"He did it!" Connie Ketchum jagged an accusing finger at the bewildered Stan. "He killed her! Lordy Mercy, I could hear the poor child screaming her head off over here, just before the dust storm blew in."

"Do you deny that, Mr. Jessup?" Detective Joe Harding asked, hoping for an easy confession.

Stan stared in pale-faced shock at the heap of broken bones and damaged flesh that he had intended on sleeping with that night. The flame of desire he had been carrying for so long went cold and, in its place, lingered a sick sensation in the pit of his stomach. "Huh? What are you getting at?"

"Our abuse center has received a few complaints concerning you, Mr. Jessup," the other detective, Terry Moore, told him. "Seems that your stepdaughter has been coming to school looking like she's been in a dogfight. Now, it isn't our place to go telling a man how to discipline his children, but this has gone beyond discipline, hasn't it, Mr. Jessup? This is downright cold-blooded murder."

A cold fear lanced through Stan Jessup's lanky frame as he looked from the three policemen to the twisted body of Becky Mae. *Why didn't that thing kill me?* he had been wondering since his awakening. *Why did it let me live?* Now he knew.

"Look, Mom!" piped Tony Ketchum, pointing out across the desert. "Will you look at that!"

They all looked. Not more than a hundred yards away hovered a lonely dust devil, bouncing back and forth between clumps of mesquite and prickly pear. But, no, as they continued to watch, the twister split and suddenly became *two*. The twin sand spouts separated, then joined, like two wistful lovers in union.

I love youuuuu, the wind seemed to whisper and a fleeting, high-pitched whistle, like the voice of a teenage girl, returned the sentiment.

They stood and watched the two dust devils as they drifted slowly across the border, blending into the dusky horizon, then vanishing. Everyone beside the trailer grew strangely silent, except for Detective Moore, who finished reading Stanley Jessup his rights.

BETTER THAN BREADCRUMBS

THEY DID NOT FOOL him with their innocence. His intense paranoia made him privy to their secret desires. Unsavory desires. Sure, they appeared harmless enough, regarding him benevolently with tiny, map-pin eyes, singing their sweet songs and hopping gingerly across the freshly mown grass. He knew that it was all a clever deception however, a lie tucked neatly inside feathered skulls, hidden within miniscule brains no larger than a wad of chewing gum.

Troy Saunders hated birds because he feared them.

But, perhaps fear was too lucid a term to describe the depth of his feelings. Mortification was more like it. The Hitchcock film had planted that awful seed of enlightenment. It had opened his youthful eyes at the tender age of seven and revealed the true nature of those foul-spirited fowls.

Since that late-show viewing, the phobia had only worsened, transcending childhood and adolescence. His sleep was invaded by horrid nightmares conjured from the images of that accursed movie: dive-bombing seagulls interrupting a birthday party game of blind man's bluff; stone hearths vomiting forth gorge upon gorge of panicked sparrows; old men lying askew in their beds, their empty eye sockets staring blankly, laced with rivulets of blood.

As he grew older, the roots of his ornithophobia strengthened and burrowed ever deeper into the fertile earth of his psyche, anchoring firmly as he approached adulthood. His shuddering horror found an outlet in cruelty. Acts of hostile retaliation and barbarity were performed upon the tiny creatures. Birds were clipped of their wing feathers and fed to the cat, while Grandmother Saunder's yellow canary was drowned beneath sudsy dishwater. Others had been blinded and maimed with the aid of his trusty BB gun at the age of twelve. His maturity only brought about more inventive ways of torment. His latest action had taken place during the final semester at Georgia State. His roommate's pet mynah, who could voice nothing but a steady stream of expletives and abusive language, had inexplicably been seized by a fit of convulsions so intense that the bird had regurgitated his own entrails. The owner had been too grief stricken to search out the cause. If he had, he might have discovered that the mynah's seed had been doctored with a potent mixture of rat poison and Drano.

Now it was the height of spring break, and the atrocities of young Troy continued. Instead of heading south to the white sands and glistening, tanned girl-flesh of the Florida beaches, he had decided to hang out at his parents' estate. In fact, his mother and father were gone to Atlanta for the day, leaving him to do as he pleased... free to vent his sadistic tendencies without the overbearing shadow of parental authority there, to damper the festivities.

It was well past noon when Troy stretched out on a lounge chair beside the kidney-shaped pool out back, soaking up some rays and inflicting explosive death. He applied a little sunscreen, sipped on a Coke and rum, and then, thumbing another cartridge into the breech and locking the bolt, lazily lifted his father's Weatherby to eye level.

The big-game rifle felt good and heavy, solid with fatal authority, as he laid his oily face against the flat of the hardwood stock and sighted down on his target. In the magnified screen of the Bushnell scope, Troy watched the activity beneath the ivy-covered fence at the far end of the pool.

A group of curious and hungry songbirds congregated around a tin pie plate

heaped with breadcrumbs and table scraps: robins, a couple of purple martins, a sassy blue jay. *Just look at the filthy buggers*, thought Troy, a shudder of revulsion running down his spine. They appeared so convincingly dumb, so contented with a simple sip of water here, a sunflower seed there, maybe a nice juicy bug every now and then. But they didn't fool him. He could see through their façade, could sense their underlying hunger. It was a nasty little hunger, one that no one really expected of them. It was a hunger for stringy strips of throbbing flesh gouged by needled talons... a hunger for the exposed spheres of human eyes, waiting to be pierced by darting beaks.

Troy waited patiently for the right one to come along, and after a while, the right one did. He hugged the bolt-action close like a blued-steel lover, his finger resting lightly upon the trigger. With a small grin of cruel pleasure, he centered the crosshairs on a gray bird with white-tipped plumage, and fired.

A .458 Magnum slug, originally intended for elephant and water buffalo, entered the bird's satiny breast, expanding, exploding the unsuspecting fowl into a bloody tangle of torn flesh and flying feathers. The other birds immediately took flight, retreating to the refuge of the surrounding trees before the bullwhip crack of the big rifle even began to fade.

"You are a very sick young man," said a voice dripping with pure disgust. Troy looked over to see the caramel-hued face of Old Miguel, the new gardener, glaring at him from over the partially trimmed hedge. The boy laid the smoking gun aside and freshened his drink with a bottle of Bacardi he had liberated from his father's liquor cabinet.

"Oh, you really think so?" Troy asked, secretly hoping to prod the elderly Cuban into heated provocation.

"Yes, I certainly do. Do you not know that it is a sin to kill a mockingbird?" scolded Miguel, sounding like Gregory Peck in that old movie about the two kids and Boo Radley. "Do you not know that they are harmless? That they do nothing but provide sweet music for us all to enjoy?"

Troy wanted to tell the old coot to mind his own business, but said nothing for a few long moments. Then he eyed the groundskeeper from behind dark shades, a crafty grin on his tanned face. "Tell me, Miguel, what is your favorite bird?"

The gardener was puzzled by the young man's question. His swarthy features hardened as he continued his pruning, then softened slightly. "I would have to say the flamingo. I lived in Florida my first years in America, and I always admired the beauty of the bird. So graceful, like a ballerina, and yet so fragile, like the bloom of a delicate flower."

Troy chuckled and again sighted through the eyepiece of the high-powered scope. "I wish I had myself one of those fancy flamingoes here right now. I'd take much pleasure in blowing its head clean off its skinny pink neck." As an added intimidation, he turned the muzzle of the empty rifle toward the elderly man, stitched the crosshairs of the scope across the gardener's angry face, and said "Bang!"

Old Miguel looked as if he might leap over the hedge and take his shears to the insolent young man. "Who do you think you are to pass judgment upon the most passive and beautiful of God's creations? You, Mr. Troy Saunders, with your moussed hair and designer clothes, your Porsche and your stock portfolio! I don't believe you would be so quick to perform such horrible acts if your father was made aware of your deviant behavior..."

The college student sat up. He pushed his sunglasses to the top of his head and gave the Cuban a warning look. "You listen up, you old fart. If you utter so much as a single word of my poolside activities to either one of my parents, I swear I'll have you fired and your work visa revoked so fast that it will make your head spin. You'll be back in Castro country before you can say Bay of Pigs."

The old man showed only contempt in the face of young Troy's threat. He snipped away a few last obtrusive twigs, then stomped off toward the little bungalow that stood adjacent to the main house on the Saunders' multi-acre property.

Troy had himself a laugh over that little confrontation, then stretched out in the July sun, sipping his rum and waiting. It would take a while for the birds to get over their gun-shyness and return to the plate of scraps. But, strangely enough, he didn't have to wait very long. A few minutes later, his attention was drawn by the noisy fluttering of wings.

"CAW!"

He looked up, and instantly his heart quickened. Standing alone before the scrap pan was the biggest, blackest crow Troy had ever laid eyes on. It was about eighteen inches from the tip of its ebony tail to the point of its equally dark beak. It looked at the plate of bird-bait, then stared at Troy. Its eyes were like pools of liquid tar, possessing an almost taunting disdain. "CAW!" it said once more, before grasping the rim of the plate with its beak, and with a flip of its massive head, dumping the contents into the short-cropped grass.

"Oh, you're really asking for it now," said Troy beneath his breath. He retrieved the rifle slowly, so as not to spook the bird, reloaded, and lifted it to his shoulder. He settled the crosshairs unerringly on the crow's temple. "Thus quote the raven...Nevermore."

He squeezed the trigger, relishing the explosive report and the bruising mule-kick of the recoil against his right shoulder. He lowered the rifle, expecting to witness the crow's headless body lying amid a snowfall of blood-speckled breadcrumbs.

"CAW!" taunted the blackbird, eyeing him with an expression akin to amusement.

"No way I could've missed," muttered Troy. "I had the sono-fabitch dead to rights!" He swiftly reloaded, shouldered the weapon, and fired. The jacketed bullet, aimed directly at the crow's shiny black breast, kicked up a geyser of dust a couple of feet to the rear.

"CAW!"

Troy was enraged. "I should have hit him, dammit! Should have blown him to smithereens!" He stood up for a better aim this time. After going through the process of reloading, he again brought the gun into line. Troy settled in the sights and saw...nothing. "Where the hell did he go?"

His answer came instantly and directly behind his left ear.

"CAW!"

He whirled in sudden, heart-thumping panic, the rifle shooting its load harmlessly skyward. The ugly thing was upon him in a flash, beating at his head with night-black wings, squawking and pecking and raking at him with sharp talons. Troy let out a feminine shriek of alarm. As he tried to escape the raven's wrath, his feet became entangled in the lounge chair. With a lurch, he was dumped into the fluoridated water of the swimming pool, expensive firearm and all.

Troy resurfaced, sputtering and swearing, in time to see the raven winging its way over the roof of the main house.

"CAW! CAW! CAW!" it cried almost laughingly, then was gone.

The humiliating attack of the monster crow returned to haunt Troy Saunders later that day, ruining his evening in more ways than one.

First of all, the drenching dump into the pool had aggravated his delicate sinus condition. He had been invited to a beer party by some of his college buddies in Atlanta that night, but he knew he would turn out to be a real drag with the blinding headache that had gripped him mercilessly by six o'clock. He lay down in his darkened bedroom after supper, listening to the echoes of laughter and conversation drifting up from the poolside terrace below. His parents were throwing a little get-together for some of their high-society friends: mostly corporate executives, a state senator or two, and their prim and proper wives.

Then, as if the pounding ache behind his cheekbones and eyes wasn't enough, he fell asleep around eight-thirty and had a dream. One of those dreams...about birds.

He found himself sitting on a bench opposite the playground of a quaint two-story schoolhouse. He felt disoriented, for the setting and the distinctive tang of saltwater in the air was strangely familiar. The faint sound of children singing "Risselty-Rosselty, now, now, now..." inside the white clapboard building stirred unpleasant emotions.

Suddenly, he knew. He stared at the weathered sign over the curved archway of the entrance. It read Bodega Bay School.

He watched uneasily as Tippi Hedren, blonde and poised, took a bench opposite him, her back to the playground. She didn't notice as the first crow lit on an upper tier of the skeletal jungle gym.

Troy wanted to warn her, but found that he was unable to do so. He could only sit there passively and observe.

Tippi took a cigarette from a case, lit it, and began to have a leisurely smoke... still unaware of the activity taking place behind her. There were four birds perched there now, staring skyward, waiting for their confederates to show.

Look behind you! he wanted to scream. *Look at all those birds!* But she seemed as oblivious to his presence as she was to the crows.

The maddening repetition of that childish song continued inside the schoolhouse. The young lady in the fashionable pea-green outfit continued her smoking, then, upon chance, glanced toward the heavens to see a single pitch-black raven circling overhead. Slowly, she followed its progress as it made a deliberate surge earthward to join the multitude gathered patiently upon swings and seesaws. *Now is your chance,* Troy thought, powerless to move or speak. *Get up slowly and make your way to the schoolhouse. Hurry now, the song has ended... they will be going out for recess soon. Go inside and warn Suzanne Pleshette and the children. Make like a fire drill and exit the building carefully, but quietly. Head down the hill, toward town...*

As if reading his mind, the woman got up and walked to the building. Troy sat there and waited nervously, his ears straining for the first sound of children's feet pounding the pavement. Yes, he could hear them now... and so could the birds. As one, they took flight, darkening the sky like a boiling storm cloud.

But they did not soar around the peak of the schoolhouse to descend, pecking and clawing, at frightened children. No, they headed in an entirely different direction this time. Across the road... straight for him.

He couldn't move, couldn't scream, couldn't do one damned thing but sit there as the churning flock engulfed him, hungrily, savagely picking his immobile body clean, peeling away flesh and sinew, right down to the bare bones.

Troy awoke with a scream lodged midway in his throat. He choked it off before it could emerge. "Damn!" he cursed, his body shivering and bathed in cold sweat. "What a nightmare that was!"

He sat on the edge of his bed for a while, before he noticed that the room was pitch black. Totally dark and totally silent. No sounds of partying echoed from the terrace below. "Must be pretty late." He glanced at the digital clock on the nightstand, but the glowing red numerals were not visible.

Shakily, Troy stood up; the pain behind his eyes was now only a dull throbbing ache. He stumbled to the door, felt for the light switch, snapped it on. Nothing happened. Still inky darkness. "The power must be off," he concluded.

But he knew that was not the case as he turned toward the open window at the far side of his bedroom. He could feel a warm, humid breeze blowing in, but the square of pale nocturnal light that should have been there was nonexistent. There was only a dense wall of impenetrable darkness every way he turned.

"What is this crap?" he muttered. He placed his hands absently to his face and found it wet, not with sweat, but with something much warmer and thicker. His hands came away sticky... and there was that peculiar smell. The hot copper stench of fresh blood.

His heart pounded in his chest and he began to hyperventilate as he reluctantly returned his hands to his face. Slowly, his fingers slid up the gore-slickened cheeks and abruptly discovered the awful source of his night-blindness. They sank to the knuckles in gaping, warm-wet holes on either side of his nose. The frayed ends of severed optic nerves teased his fingertips before he could withdraw them in sickening horror.

"Oh God... my eyes!" he moaned in despair. "They pecked out my freaking eyes!"

Panic overcame him. He stumbled sightlessly into the outer hallway, making his way to his parents' room. He threw open the door, hands outstretched, feeling for their bed. "Mom... Dad... you gotta help me... my eyes... gone... call an ambulance!" He received no reply to his frantic sobs. Troy reached the bed and found no one there. In fact, it was still made. The blanket and sheets hadn't even been turned down for the night.

"Mom... Dad?" He staggered back into the hallway, groping for direction. Then, from the stairway came a sound. A rusty, shrill sound that made Troy's blood run cold with fear and dread.

"CAW!"

"So it was *you*. You black bastard!" he bellowed. "It was you who did this to me!" He reached for the hall table and located the heavy brass candlestick he knew was there. With a heave, he threw it in the general direction of the bird. It struck the stained-glass window at the head of the staircase, shattering it loudly.

There was a stretch of silence, then the fluttering of oily wings as the cursed fowl made its way downstairs.

"CAW!" it called invitingly.

Troy found the stairway and worked his way downward as he clutched at the sturdy, oaken banister. "Where are you?" he yelled. "Where, dammit?"

From his dad's study. "CAW!"

He stumbled, feet dragging across the expensive Oriental rug; then he slid open the double doors. He carefully skirted the leather-upholstered furnishings, felt along the walls with their carved mahogany bookcases laden with old and priceless volumes. "Don't be such a coward!" he said vehemently. "I know you're in here!"

Then the sound of pumping wings cut swiftly across the study, disappearing through the open French doors that led onto the terrace. Troy reached the doorway, afraid that the open air had secured his enemy's release. He was on the verge of bellowing a curse of anguish, when the small sounds of mass movement froze him. He stood perfectly still and listened.

The backyard was full of them, teaming with patiently perched blackbirds like those on the school playground at Bodega Bay. He clutched the doorframe in terror, afraid to move a muscle or utter a sound that might draw their attention. Then, finally, he gathered his nerve and ducked back into the study.

He fumbled along the wall until he found the huge antique gun cabinet. He opened the doors, his bloody hands traveling from one longarm to the next. The Weatherby wouldn't do this time. He needed something with a little more punch and spread to it. Yes, this would do it... the Remington pump. He took the shotgun from its rack, then rummaged through the lower drawers of the cabinet for the correct ammunition.

After loading the gun with twelve-gauge shells, he stepped boldly out onto the terrace, the flagstones cool against his bare feet. "Here I am, you filthy creatures!" he growled. "Come and get me!"

"CAW?" inquired a bird to his right. He shouldered the gun and unleashed a booming hail of double-ought buckshot. He heard the dying squawk and the sound of a canopied patio table crashing to its side.

Suddenly, the yard was alive with the sounds of cawing and the flapping of airborne wings. Troy pumped the shotgun and fired, saturating the air with lead pellets.

"CAW! CAW! CAW!" shrieked the panicked fowls. He could sense their torn bodies plummeting as they crashed onto the smooth hardness of the terrace stones. "CAW!" yelped one to his left. He fired another round. The bird hit the pool with a resounding splash. Cripes, that was a big one, thought Troy with satisfaction.

He heard a number of them winging their way toward the rear gate. Three more shots dispatched them neatly before they could make their escape.

He worked the slide again and found that his last shell had been spent. But it no longer mattered. The job was finished.

"I got them... got them all."

Troy found an overturned patio chair and sat there in his new state of permanent darkness. He breathed in the fresh night air, sweet with the scent of death, and cherished the complete and utter silence... at least until the sirens approached by way of Atlanta.

"It's a real mess back there," the police officer told the detective on duty. "Bodies all over the place. Looks like the kid went berserk... killed his folks and all their high-class friends."

The detective regarded the blood-splattered young man who sat handcuffed in the rear of the patrol car. "My eyes," muttered Troy Saunders. "How could they have done such a thing? My poor, poor eyes..."

The two policemen exchanged questioning looks, then shrugged. They couldn't figure out what the kid was mumbling about. His eyes looked perfectly okay to them. He had to be a real nut case.

"So, you heard the shooting... and then what?" the detective asked, continuing his questioning of the crime's only witness.

Old Miguel shook his head sadly. "I ran from my bungalow, looked over the hedge, and there he was, young Mr. Troy, standing over all those poor people with a shotgun. It was horrible... very tragic."

"Yes," agreed the cop. He turned to his partner. "Officer Tanner, you'd better get on the radio and call the coroner's office. Looks like this little massacre is going to take all night to clean up."

As the police went about their business, Miguel slipped away, heading around the side of the main house, toward the terrace. When he reached the fence, he peered at the shot-riddled bodies that lay sprawled and stiffening upon the bloodstained tiles, a couple of them floating face down in the cloudy water of the pool. The overhead patio lights cast an eerie glow upon the awful carnage.

Miguel stared at the sickening scene for a long moment, but not with grief or shock. No, a peculiar expression of great satisfaction creased his dark-skinned features. That and a look of intense, carrion-like *hunger*.

The old man lifted his eyes—eyes as black and shiny as those of a raven—to the dark foliage of the surrounding trees. He smiled an almost fatherly smile and softly, whispered a single word.

"Caw."

They descended from the trees, hundreds of them. A massive, churning flock of crows, cardinals, bluebirds, finches, birds of all sizes and species. They glided as one from the thick summer greenery and covered the seventeen carcasses like gently falling leaves. They made no sound that might alert the policemen out front. They knew it would be a good half hour or so before the others arrived and began to sort through the mess the bird-hater had unknowingly committed that night.

Until then, they would enjoy a far better feast than that which mere breadcrumbs could provide.

ROMOCIDE

THEY WERE due for a bad one.

The '96 Olympics had come and gone, leaving everyone on the force expecting the floodgates to open. During the festivities, it appeared the entire city of Atlanta had been on its best behavior. With the exception of the Centennial Park bombing, crime as a whole had reached an unnerving low. Of course, vice had been busy with streetwalkers and pickpockets, but muggings and violent crime had seemingly dropped from the books. The eyes of the world had focused on Atlanta and, if only for a while, it was as if the local low-life population had kicked back in front of the TV with a cold beer, watching the show with everyone else.

But that was over now. The Atlanta PD's homicide division had its hands full once again.

It was a night in mid-September when Lowery and Taylor got the call. They pulled their white Chrysler off Peachtree Street and into a well-to-do apartment complex called Tara Court. They drove past the main office — which resembled a miniature version of Scarlett O'Hara's famous mansion — then cruised down the winding avenues of the complex itself. Half of the buildings were standard flat-type apartments, three stories tall, while the others consisted of townhouses, all decorated in the same *Gone With The Wind* motif.

"Pretty original, isn't it?" said Sergeant Ed Taylor.

"Tacky is more like it," replied Lieutenant Ken Lowery. "I mean, look at the names of the streets. Rhett Butler Avenue, Ashley Wilkes Drive, Aunt Pitty-Pat Lane. It's a little overdone, if you ask me."

His partner shrugged and spotted the telltale flash of blue and red emergency lights coming from Mammy Boulevard up head. "Maybe. But this *is* Atlanta. And

it *is* better than a *Wizard of Oz* theme, you've got to admit that."

"I suppose so," agreed Lowery. He could imagine such a complex with an office that resembled the Emerald City and apartments that were patterned after Munchkinland.

They parked in a space outside a line of townhouses. Each had its own distinctive form of Southern architecture. Two patrol cars and a metro fire engine were already there, as well as Stuart White's maroon station wagon. Four out of five times, the city coroner beat them to the scene of the crime, which was kind of funny considering that Stu Walsh is nearly seventy years old.

"That's it over there," said Lowery, pointing to a townhouse with white brick and immaculate Roman columns framing its doorway. "Apartment 503."

The two homicide detectives left the car and crossed the sidewalk to the townhouse. A border of yellow police tape had been erected around 503, but there were no curious bystanders lingering beyond it, like at most crime scenes. But then this was a complex that catered mostly to young professional types who were apparently more discreet with their rubber-necking than most spectators were. On further inspection, they could make out the silhouettes of the neighboring residents in the lighted windows of their apartments, wondering what type of sordid occurrence had taken place in their clean, crime-free complex.

A police officer stood beside the open door of Apartment 503, talking to a firefighter. "Officer Mangrum," Lowery said in greeting.

The young patrolman seemed grateful that he had been remembered. "How are you doing, Lieutenant?" He nodded to the other detective. "Sergeant?"

"We're doing fine, Mangrum," said Lowery. "So what do we have here?"

The officer frowned. "We're not exactly sure, sir. It's pretty weird."

Lowery looked at Taylor. "Then I reckon we'd better take a look at it ourselves."

"My partner, Robinson, is upstairs with Dr. Walsh. It's the bedroom to your right."

"Thanks." The two entered the cramped but stylish foyer of the townhouse. As they passed through the doorway, they noticed that the front door had been pried open. The wood around the deadbolt was splintered. They mounted the narrow stairway. As they approached the upper floor, they immediately detected a cloying odor. An odor that was nearly sickening in nature.

"Smells like burnt barbecue," said Taylor.

"More like a burnt body to me," his partner said. "Remember that case over in the projects? When that woman set fire to her drunk of a husband after he'd raped their ten-year-old daughter? Smells kind of like that bastard did, after she got through with him."

Taylor nodded. "You're right. But this smells even *worse*."

When they reached the head of the stairs, Lowery called out. "Stu?"

"In here, Ken," replied the coroner's gravelly voice.

Lowery and Taylor stepped into the bedroom, which was really no bedroom at all. It looked to have been used more as an office than anything else. Stark black-and-white Ansel Adams prints decorated the walls. Beneath them were several file cabinets and a large Ricoh copier; the type that high-volume offices use. Against one wall was a stereo system and two speakers, as well as a rack of classical CDs. At the wall directly opposite was a large computer work center, complete with an IBM system with a Pentium microprocessor and a state-of-the-art laser printer.

But the surroundings of the upstairs room paled in comparison to the central focal point, which was directly in front of the computer desk. It was a dark, scorched patch that stretched across the neutral gray carpeting. The two couldn't see it very well at first. Stu Walsh was crouched on the floor, obscuring their view.

"What have we got here, Stu?" Lowery asked.

"The damnedest thing I've ever seen," said the coroner.

When Walsh stood up and stepped aside, they saw exactly what was on the carpet. At first, their minds balked at what they were looking at. It seemed utterly impossible. Then, slowly, it dawned on them that what lay before them was for real.

The carpet wasn't scorched after all. Rather, an outline of powdery black ash covered the floor. An outline that was undeniably *human* in form.

But that wasn't all there was to it. Within the outline was a blackened pair of eyeglasses with melted plastic lenses, several human teeth, some with fillings, and a steel surgical pin where the outline of one leg was. A computer chair lay on its side next to the outline. The seat and back cushions were charred down to the foam padding, but little of the chrome framework had been scorched.

Lowery and Taylor may have thought the whole thing was some elaborate practical joke someone had pulled, except for one factor. At the end of the outline's left arm was part of an actual human limb. The hand and forearm of a man lay there. It was clad in the sleeve of a white sweatshirt, only the upper end of which was scorched. From where they stood, they could see that the stub of arm seemed to have been burnt off, rather than severed. And the stump appeared to have been cauterized by some intense and inexplicable heat.

"Good Lord," said Taylor. "What is it?"

"Well, it may sound crazy," said Stu Walsh. "But I believe it's the remains of a young man."

Lowery looked doubtful. "You mean the one who lived here?" He turned to Officer Robinson. "What was his name?"

Robinson stepped forward, looking pale and shaken. "Phillip Bomar. He'd lived here for three years." He handed the lieutenant a black leather wallet. "I found this on the nightstand in the master bedroom."

Lowery opened the wallet and studied a Georgia state driver's license. From the information there, he gathered that Phillip Bomar had been twenty-six years old and was five feet, nine inches tall. The photograph showed a lean, young man with longish brown hair and pale green eyes. He wore eyeglasses identical to the scorched frames that lay within the parameter of the outline's ashen head.

"I don't understand," he said. "You're saying that *this* is Bomar?'

"I'm saying that it's *probably* Bomar," said Walsh. "I can't say for sure just yet."

"The hand's wearing a college ring," said Taylor. "Looks like it's from the University of Georgia."

Stu Walsh pointed to a framed diploma on the wall. "Bomar attended UG. But that doesn't prove for certain that it's him."

"But what the hell happened to him? Did some psycho take a flame-thrower to him?"

"That's very unlikely," the coroner explained. "If that was the case, there would be traces of chemicals and fuel here. There isn't. And the entire apartment would have gone up in flames. As you can see, it didn't."

Lowery took a step closer to the computer desk, careful not to tread on the bizarre outline of black ashes. He suddenly noticed that some incredible heat had been generated directly where the outline lay. The gray-white plastic housing of the computer monitor and microprocessor had buckled and melted, and the monitor screen was cloudy and cracked. The keyboard had melted so badly that all the keys were practically fused together.

Taylor looked down at the mouse, which sat on a charred rubber pad beside the keyboard. Clots of gummy soot spotted the oval instrument. "What's this black stuff?" he asked Walsh.

"Burnt flesh," he replied grimly. "Looks like the guy was holding onto it when it happened."

"That's the big question," said Lowery, shaking his head. "Exactly what *did* happen?"

The coroner looked as though he was reluctant to answer. He sighed, then went ahead. "Have either of you ever heard of spontaneous human combustion?"

Taylor laughed, but it was a nervous laugh. "Sure, but that's just a load of bull, isn't it? Things like that don't really happen."

"There have been documented cases," Walsh told him.

"Yeah, but this isn't the freaking X-Files," Lowery said. "And we're not Mulder and Scully." He searched the coroner's face. "Don't you have any other explanation? One that's not so unbelievable?"

"I'll let you know after I complete my examination of the remains back at the lab." It was obvious that no conventional autopsy could be performed. "But, as of right now, spontaneous combustion seems to be the apparent cause of death."

Lowery and Taylor stared at the ashy outline for a long moment. "Okay," said the lieutenant. "Let's get all the evidence we can while the scene is secure. Get Blakely over here with a forensic team. I want him to go over everything in this room with a fine-tooth comb. And I want plenty of pictures. Call Jenny Burke and have her snap a couple rolls of the body — if you can call it that — as well as the contents of this room. If I have to turn in a report to the chief that says this Phillip Bomar went in flames for no reason at all, I want plenty of evidence and photos to back it up."

Lowery left the upstairs room and called Robinson into the outer hallway. The police officer gave him a quick rundown of what had transpired. A smoke detector in Apartment 503 had gone off, alerting Bomar's next door neighbor, who called 911. The firemen had pried the front door open — whose deadbolt had been locked from the inside — then proceeded upstairs. There was a light mist of smoke, along with the heavy scent of scorched plastic and burnt flesh. When the firefighters discovered the strange outline on the carpet, they called in the Atlanta PD.

Feeling drained and more than a little confused, the two detectives left Apartment 503. They climbed into their car, but simply sat there in front of the townhouse for a while.

"I'm not even sure if this is a homicide, Ed," said Lowery. "It seems more like an unexplained death to me."

"I think there's foul play involved somewhere down the line," Taylor told him. "I don't know why yet…"

Lowery nodded solemnly. "You and me both. It's creepy, isn't it?"

"I'll say," agreed his partner. "Even creepier than those murders Dwight Rollins pulled a few years back."

Lowery shuddered. He vividly recalled the crazy, old blind man who had murdered several people in his apartment building – as well as his own seeing-eye dog. And for what reason? Because it was the dead of winter and he needed their warm eyes to fill empty sockets that his pawned glass eyes had left behind.

"I never thought we'd see one that beat the Rollins case," he said, starting up the car. "But I guess I was wrong."

The next morning, Lowery and Taylor came in to find a message waiting for them. It was from a Doctor James Arendale. All the doctor said was that his call concerned Phillip Bomar. He had left his office address and requested that they see him as soon as possible.

When they arrived at Arendale's downtown office, they were surprised to find the words 'clinical psychologist' beneath his name on the door. They had just assumed that he was a physician of the body, rather than one of the mind.

Arendale was a tall, lean man with graying brown hair and a neatly trimmed beard. He shook their hands, then motioned to two chairs located before his desk. "Please, have a seat."

When they had one so, Doctor Arendale paused, then began to speak. "I am surrendering the restrictions of patient confidentially on the request of Phillip Bomar's parents. They felt it might assist you in your investigation if I were to clarify exactly who and what poor Phillip was."

"So Phillip Bomar was a patient of yours?" asked Lowery.

"Yes," for nearly twenty-two of his twenty-six years."

"Was he mentally unstable?" asked Taylor.

"In a sense, yes. But in another sense... well, this is sort of difficult to explain. If I don't phrase this carefully, it might actually sound crazy and impossible to you."

"In light of what we saw last night," said Lowery, "I don't think we'd consider

anything crazy and impossible."

The psychologist was silent for a moment, privately choosing his words. "Phillip suffered from a very rare mental/physical condition. He was a stigmachondriac."

"A *what?*" asked Taylor. "I don't believe I've ever heard that term before."

"That's because it is one of my own making," said Arendale with a half-smile. He regarded the two homicide detectives opposite him. "Do you know what the phenomenon of *stigmata* is?"

"Sure," said Lowery. "That's when someone's body plays tricks on them due to some devout belief, mostly of a religious nature. Like someone bleeding from the hands and feet in imitation of Christ's crucifixion."

"Correct," agreed Arendale. "But there are some cases of non-religious stigmata as well. People exhibiting an inflamed handprint in remembrance of a childhood beating, or women exhibiting all the physical characteristics of pregnancy, simply because they believe it to be so."

"And Phillip Bomar was like that?"

"To the extreme. Since the age of four, Phillip exhibited numerous episodes of stigmata. His mind and body were always at a constant war with one another. He could watch TV, see a child being beaten on a show, then dream about the incident and wake up with identical bruises. Once he had a nightmare of falling off a cliff and woke up screaming with a broken leg. He had to have surgical pins implanted in his knee for that episode.

"His parents were suspected of child abuse at first, but then I was called in. I kept him under clinical observation for a period of time. It was horrifying and, yes, I admit, professionally intriguing, to watch burns and abrasions appear on a body that had been assaulted only in the mind."

"Was that the extent of Phillip's phenomena?" asked Lowery. "Bruises and broken bones?"

"No," said Arendale. "He could just as easily be tricked into thinking that he was suffering an illness, even a fatal one. Once a team of doctors even believed that he was suffering from advanced leukemia. But once I convinced Phillip otherwise, the symptoms of the cancer disappeared completely. And then there was the matter of the gunshot."

"Gunshot?"

The doctor explained. "When he was a teenager, he and several of his friends went to see a movie, one of the Dirty Harry films I believe it was. When they left the theater and were walking down the sidewalk, a passing car backfired. The noise frightened Phillip. His mind kicked in, convincing him that a gun had been fired. He fell to the ground, bleeding from a large hole in his shoulder. When he was wheeled into surgery, they sutured a wound the exact size that a .44 magnum round would make. You see, his mind was convinced that he had been shot, and so his body reacted to the suggestion. He nearly died from that one."

Lieutenant Lowery sat there quietly for a moment. "So what you're saying is Phillip was probably killed by his own mind and body?"

"Yes," said Arendale. "If, in fact, it *was* Phillip Bomar's remains you found."

Taylor nodded grimly. "It was. We got a positive ID from the coroner this morning. The fingerprints on the surviving hand matched Bomar's prints precisely."

"That's what I was afraid of," said Arendale. He sank back in his leather chair. "Tell me, exactly how did Phillip die? I haven't been able to find out so far."

Lowery didn't think it would do any harm to tell him. "He was totally incinerated by some unknown catalyst. Do you believe it could have been self-generated?"

"Yes, I'm certain that it could have."

"Tell me this," he continued. "Could it have been suicide?"

Dr. Arendale shook his head. "No, that is out of the question. Phillip had problems, but he had a great zest and love for living. That was the main reason he survived such a chain of severe occurrences. Also, he had done much to insulate himself against experiencing his stigmatic tendencies."

"What do you mean 'insulate' himself?" asked Taylor.

"Did you notice anything strange when you were in his apartment last night? Phillip did not own a television set. He purposely limited his exposure to TV programs, as well as newscasts. The violence he saw on television was potentially dangerous to him. He stopped going to movie theaters for the same reason. And he purified his musical tastes as well. You may have noticed that he listened only to classical music. Music with absolutely *no* lyrics. If he had listened to rock or rap music, the lyrics alone could have actually killed him."

"Damn," said Taylor beneath his breath. "Then the poor kid was like a walking time bomb. But only to himself."

"I couldn't have said it any better," Arendale told him. "But Phillip took great pains to isolate himself from such influences. He was a computer genius and he worked at home, processing data for various corporations. He made quite a comfortable living at it, too. Incidentally, his only interests were listening to classical music and playing non-confrontational computer games. He didn't even read books, afraid of what the printed word might conjure inside his psyche."

"Did he have friends? A girlfriend perhaps?"

"No. Unfortunately, Phillip was something of a recluse. He had no social life whatsoever. He was afraid of loving another human being. He actually feared that rejection might cause something within him that could not be mended with steel pins or stitches."

"So what you're saying, doctor, is that Phillip's death was due to no fault of his own," clarified Lowery.

"That's what I'm saying, Lieutenant." The psychologist stared at

Lowery and his partner somberly. "I believe in my heart that Phillip was murdered. Murdered by someone who knew precisely what he was. And, with that knowledge, used his own condition against him. Yes, someone murdered him, just as sure as if they'd shot him with a gun or stabbed him with a knife."

On their way back to the office, the two discussed their meeting with James Arendale.

"Was he just being melodramatic?" asked Taylor. "Or was he on the money?"

"I think he's on the right track," said Lowery. "I'm actually beginning to believe that someone turned Phillip Bomar against himself and caused him to spontaneously combust."

"Maybe Blakely has something for us in Forensics," said Taylor.

He did. When they walked into the lab, Tom Blakely looked excited, the way he always did when he had discovered some particularly damning piece of evidence. "Just the guys I've been waiting for," he said with a big grin on his face.

"Looks like you found something," said Lowery.

"Several things, in fact," said Blakely. "From the crime scene, we've gathered that Bomar was sitting in front of his computer, right?"

"Right."

"Well, I was curious as to exactly *what* he was doing at the moment of his death," said the forensics expert. "So, I asked to have his computer brought to the lab. And look what I found in the CD-ROM drive after I pried the drawer loose."

He handed them a CD-ROM in a protective evidence bag. Taylor read the title on the silver disk: *You Are There... Famous Disasters!* "So exactly what is it?"

"Well, as you know, I'm something of a computer buff myself," said Blakely. "This is an interactive CD-ROM in which the participant experiences actual historical disasters, both natural and man-made."

Lowery looked at Taylor, thinking the same thing. "Interesting. So what sort of disasters are on this disk?"

"Tornados, earthquakes, mostly stuff like that," he told them. "But then there are others, like the crash of the Hindenburg and the atomic blast at Hiroshima."

"Sounds like either one of them could have done the trick," said Taylor.

"No, I believe it was another program entirely that killed Mr. Bomar," said Blakely. He walked toward a computer in an adjoining office. "Step this way, gentlemen."

"Talk about melodramatic," said Lowery beneath his breath.

They watched as Blakely inserted the CD-ROM into the drive. "I've already programmed this into the system, so it's ready to go." A menu appeared on the monitor screen, displaying the choices available. Blakely used the mouse to click on the one he desired, then took them through the program. They found themselves following a line of several people dressed in pale blue coveralls with NASA patches sewn to the upper sleeves.

"I think I know where this is leading," said Taylor in amazement.

"In this particular program, you're playing the part of a particular person who was supposed to be the first civilian teacher in space," said Blakely. He followed the group with the aid of his mouse. Soon they had entered a chamber with walls and a roof covered with electronic consoles. DO YOU WISH TO PROCEED? asked a box that appeared on the screen. Blakely clicked on YES and found himself strapped into a seat with the others similarly seated around him.

Lowery and Taylor waited breathlessly as the countdown came, followed by the lift-off. A clock in the corner of the screen counted off the seconds until the expected disaster took place. Then it happened. A burst of bright light flashed at the far end of the chamber, followed by a roaring rush of pure fire as the inhabitants were fully engulfed.

"Okay, we've seen enough," said Ken Lowery. He felt as though someone had just sucker punched him in the stomach.

"It was the explosion of the space shuttle Challenger," said Taylor. "That was

what incinerated Phillip Bomar?"

"I'd stake my reputation on it," said the forensics expert.

"Well, that tells us *how*," said Lowery. "That just leaves *who* and *why*."

Blakely looked pleased with himself. "I believe I've figured that out for you, too."

"You're really earning your paycheck on this one, Tom," said the police lieutenant. "What have you got?"

He handed them a five page printout. "I found this on Bomar's hard drive. It seems that he made a record of people he communicated with through the internet on a regular basis. Just hold on to that and I'll show you something else."

They waited while he brought out a brown padded mailing envelope. "I found this in Bomar's wastebasket. I believe the killer sent him the CD-ROM in this envelope."

Taylor read the return address. "Rom Exchange. What's that?"

"It's a computer software exchange network," said Blakely. "I've used it before. You can rent CD-ROM games from this company in Seattle. They have their own website on the net."

"So does this murderer work for this Rom Exchange?"

"No. I think they forged a mailing label and sent Bomar this CD-ROM on the chance that he might use it." Again, that look of smug satisfaction. "I peeled the mailing label away and found another one underneath. The name and address had been scratched out, but it didn't take much work to lift the impressions from the envelope underneath."

Lowery looked at the name and address that had been lifted from the mailing envelope, then looked at the internet record. It was there, several dozen times in the past month. The last entry was four days ago.

Susan Graham, 577 Oceanview Drive, Jacksonville, Florida.

"But what I want to know is how come Bomar even put the disk in his system and checked it out?" asked Taylor. "He must've known how dangerous it could be."

"Maybe he was just bored," suggested Lowery. "Or curious. And, like the proverbial cat, his curiosity ended up killing him."

"But not without some help," said Blakely.

It was the following morning when they made their move, with the assistance of the Jacksonville Police Department.

"It still sounds pretty crazy to me," said Detective Art Stafford as they pulled up in front of 577 Oceanview Drive."

"I don't know, Art," said his partner, Steve Kraft. "We've had some weird cases ourselves. Remember when that teenager disappeared for three weeks and then showed up in the middle of that shopping mall, claiming he'd been abducted by aliens? And the polygraph claimed that he was telling the truth?"

"That kid was a nutcase," said Stafford.

"We're not here to argue whether this case is plausible or not," Lowery said from the backseat of their unmarked car. "We've got arrest and extradition warrants for this Susan Graham and that's what we're here for. So let's get to it."

"Okay," said Stafford. "But I hope you guys aren't making fools of yourselves."

The four men left the car and walked up the concrete sidewalk to a clapboard house painted coral pink. The front yard was decorated with pink flamingoes standing on wire legs and sea shells collected from the beach, which was just a stone's throw away.

They opened the screen door and paused for a moment, unbuttoning jackets and unfastening holsters. Then Stafford knocked on the door.

They heard someone stir inside, but no one answered the door.

He knocked louder. "Miss Graham, this is Detective Stafford of the Jacksonville Police. Please open the door… right now."

They half expected some resistance, but they were surprised.

They heard the rattle of a chain being disengaged, and then the door opened.

Susan Graham didn't look like a murder suspect. Instead, she looked like a sadder, heavier version of Phillip Bomar. Her shoulder-length hair was a lusterless red, she wore tortoise-shell glasses, and her plain face was pimply and utterly devoid of makeup. She wore a Miami Dolphins t-shirt, white shorts, and green flip-flops.

"Come in," she said softly, almost in a whisper. The two Atlanta detectives received the same impression. She was shocked and scared by their appearance on her doorstep, but there was a grim acceptance as well. In a way, she had hoped to get away with her crime scott-free, but in another, she knew that she never would.

The four policemen stepped into a cramped living room decorated with second-hand furniture and the type of framed prints you can buy at Walmart. The only point of sophistication in the entire room was a desk bearing an expensive Hewlett Packard computer and laser printer. Taste wise, it was as far from Phillip Bomar's upstairs office as you could get. But it still held the same dreary air of isolation.

"Susan Graham," said Lowery. "Were you acquainted with a Phillip Andrew Bomar?"

"Yes," said the young woman with a sigh. "But only through the internet. I never actually met him in person."

Taylor took the CD-ROM from his jacket pocket. "And did you mail Mr. Bomar this?"

Susan Graham stared at the disk for a long moment. "Yes, I did."

The lieutenant showed her the papers. "Miss Graham, I have a warrant for your arrest on the charge of the willful and premeditated murder of Phillip Bomar."

She stared at them silently, then began to back away. "Okay," she said in resignation. "I did it. I admit that. But before you take me, let me tell you *why* I did what I did."

"Maybe you ought to wait until you talk to an attorney, Miss Graham," suggested Detective Stafford. "This is a serious crime you're being charged with."

"I know how serious it is!" she snapped at him. She stopped her slow retreat and stood in the center of the living room. The computer was to her left, while a doorway leading into the back of the house stood to her right. "Just let me tell you and get it over with, okay?"

Stafford shrugged and looked over at Lowery. "It's your ball-game, pal. If she wants to talk now, that's okay with us."

Taylor took a micro-recorder from his pocket, showed it to the young woman, and turned it on. "Be advised that anything you now say can and will be used against you in a court of law."

They stood and waited, giving her time to gather her thoughts. Then Susan Graham began to talk.

"I met Phillip on the net. We were both lonely and we just sort of lucked up on each other by accident. We found we both had a lot of the same interests and started talking to each other through the computer. I fell in love with him and told him so. But then I guess he got scared. He refused to communicate with me anymore. For a couple of weeks, I left messages on his email, but he wouldn't answer them. I was crushed at first. Then I guess I sort of lost my temper."

"You were aware of his condition?" asked Lowery.

She nodded. "He told me about it a week or two after we started talking."

"And you sent him this CD-ROM out of spite? For dumping you?"

Tears began to bloom in Susan Graham's eyes. Slowly, she began to back up

toward the doorway. "Phillip was stupid! So damn stupid! He didn't know how lucky he was!"

Taylor shucked his revolver from his holster and held it at his side. "Stay where you are, Miss Graham."

But she ignored him. Step by step, she made her way toward the far end of the living room. "He didn't realize how much we had in common!" she sobbed. "He didn't realize just how much alike we were!"

"Miss Graham..." called the police sergeant, raising his gun.

Suddenly, she turned and ran through the doorway and down a short hallway to a bathroom. By the time they got there, the door had been slammed shut and locked from the inside.

"Open this door, Miss Graham," called Lowery. "Or we'll be forced to break it down."

For a moment, there was only silence. Then a long, mournful scream shrilled from the opposite side of the door.

"Let's do it!' said Taylor. He and Lowery kicked at the door three times before the door frame splintered around the lock and the door slammed inward with a crash.

The four detectives crowded through the doorway and stopped. They stood frozen in their tracks, staring at the mess on the bathroom floor.

"Oh dear God," said Lowery.

Detective Stafford's eyes grew wide with shock, unable to comprehend what he was looking at.

"What happened?" he demanded to know. *"What the hell happened to her?"*

At the request of the Jacksonville coroner, they stepped into the lab.

"There are a few points that I need to clarify before I proceed with the autopsy," he said. "This was the condition you found her in upon entering the bathroom?"

Lowery, Taylor, Stafford, and Kraft took a step closer. They stared at the naked body of Susan Graham lying on the stainless steel gurney. "Yes," Lowery said, speaking for them all.

"And it was only a matter of seconds between the time she locked the door and the time you gained entrance?"

"That's right," said Stafford.

The coroner shook his head. "I don't understand. I simply don't understand how this could have taken place in such a short period of time."

Ken Lowery and Ed Taylor stared at the fatal injuries that had taken the life of Susan Graham.

The coroner pointed them out with a rubber-gloved hand.

"Severe lacerations of both wrists, resulting in massive blood loss."

No razor blades or sharp objects had been found in the bathroom.

"Indications of strangulation and rope burns around the throat."

No rope or cord had been discovered, either.

"And this," said the coroner, shaking his head in bewilderment. "A circular wound to the right temple and severe hemorrhaging of the brain. Like a bullet hole, but with no evidence of powder burns around the opening of the wound."

They had searched the bathroom several times. Absolutely no gun had been found.

Silence hung in the room for a long moment. Then Lowery spoke. "She was right, then."

"About what?" asked Stafford.

Lowery glanced over at his partner. He could tell by the look in Taylor's eyes that he had come to the same conclusion.

"She and Phillip Bomar *were* a lot alike. But in all the wrong ways."

THINNING THE HERD

CHANEY WAITED UNTIL THE FIRST, pale hint of dawn seeped over the flat Texas horizon. Then, making sure everything was set, he descended the rusty ladder of the old water tower and made his way to the barn across the street.

He was the thirteenth in line. When his time came, he stepped up to the landlord's desk and appraised the man. He was human, that was easy to see. Fat, lazy, willing to bow to those who had taken command of the new frontier. His name was Hector. He had a patch over one eye, a prosthetic leg that needed oiling, and a monkey named Garfunkel who perched like a growth on the landlord's shoulder and picked lice from his master's oily scalp.

Hector eyed the gaunt man in the black canvas duster with suspicion. "Don't think I've ever seen you around here before."

Chaney's impatience showed as he reached into his coat for his money pouch. "You gonna flap your lips or rent me a bed for the day?" Gold coins jingled within the small leather bag like the restless bones of a ghostly child.

"How do I know you are what you say you are? There are plenty of bounty hunters about these days. Doesn't pay to rent out to strangers, especially when you cater to the type of clientele I do."

"Your clientele is going to fry out here if you don't hurry up and give the man his bed," growled a customer at the end of the line.

But Hector was not to be rushed. "I'll need proof."

Chaney smirked. "What do you want? An ID? How about my American Express card?"

The landlord reached into the desk drawer and withdrew a small, golden crucifix. "Grab hold of this."

Chaney averted his eyes, as did the others in line. "Is that necessary?"

"It is if you want a bed."

The stranger nodded and extended a pale hand. He closed his fist around the cross. A sizzling of flesh sounded as contact was made and a wisp of blue smoke curled from between Chaney's fingers. "Satisfied?" he asked in disgust.

"Quite." Hector pushed the register toward him and collected the gold piece Chaney had laid upon the counter. The one-eyed landlord noticed that Chaney carried a black satchel in one hand. "What's that?" he asked.

Chaney flashed a toothy grin. "A noonday snack." He shook the black bag, eliciting the muffled cry of an infant from within.

By the time the first rays of the sun had broken, they were all checked in. The barn's interior was pitch dark, letting nary a crack or crevice of scorching sunlight into their temporary abode. Chaney found a bed on the ground floor. He removed his long coat, hanging it on a peg over his bunk, and set the satchel close at hand.

He lifted the lid of his sleeping chamber and scowled. Just a simple, pine wood casket. No silk liner, no burnished finish, and no ornate handles on the sides; just a no frills bunk in a no frills hotel. He wasn't complaining, though. It would suit his purpose well enough.

"Lights out!" called Hector, laughing uproariously at a joke that had lost its humor years ago. The tenants ignored his mirth and set about preparing for a good day's rest. Chaney followed suit, taking a packet of graveyard earth from his coat pocket and spreading it liberally in the bottom of his rented coffin.

When every lid had been closed, Hector stepped outside the barn, shutting the double doors behind him. He took a seat on a bench out front, laid a pump shotgun across his knees, and started reading an old Anne Rice novel he had bought from a traveling peddler.

The morning drew on, the sun rising, baking the Texas wilderness with its unrelenting heat. The little town moved as slow as winter molasses. Its inhabitants went about their normal business, or as near normal as expected after the much heralded End of the World.

The courthouse clock struck twelve o'clock before Chaney finally made his move. It was safe now; his neighboring tenants were fast asleep. Quietly, he lifted the lid of this casket and sat up. "Snack time," he said to himself and reached for the satchel.

He opened it. The first thing he removed was the rubber baby doll. He laid it on the barn floor, smiling as it uttered a soft "Mama!" before falling silent again. Chaney then took a .44 AutoMag from the bag and began to make his rounds.

He didn't bother to pull the old "stake-through-the-heart" trick. To do so would be noisy and messy and net him only a small fraction of the undead he had come there to finish off. Instead, he used the most state-of-the-art anti-vampire devices. He placed Claymore mines at strategic points throughout the barn's interior. But they were not ordinary Claymores. He had replaced the load of ball bearings with tiny steel crucifixes and splinters of ash wood.

After the mines had been placed and the timers set, Chaney knew it was time to take his leave. He walked to the barn doors and, cocking his pistol, stepped out into the hot, noonday sun.

Hector was snoozing on the job, of course. The landlord's head was resting on his flabby chest, snoring rather loudly from the nose. Chaney stood before the man and loudly cleared his throat.

The fat man came awake. Startled, he stared up at Chaney. "Hey," he breathed. "You ain't no vampire."

"No, I ain't," agreed Chaney.

"But I saw your hand burn when you touched the cross!"

Chaney lifted his scarred left palm to his mouth and peeled away a thin layer of chemically treated latex with his teeth. "Special effects," he said.

"Well, I'll be damned."

Chaney brought the muzzle of his .44 to the man's forehead. "That you shall be... traitor." Then he painted the barn wall a brilliant red with the contents of the man's disintegrating skull.

The bogus vampire walked to where his primer-gray van was parked near the water tower. He got in, started the engine, and cruised slowly down the empty street of the town. He checked his watch, counting the seconds. "Five... four...three...two... one..."

The Claymores went off first. Their metal shells split under a charge of C-4, sending thousands of tiny crosses and toothpick-sized stakes in every imaginable direction. The projectiles penetrated the caskets, as well as their sleeping occupants. Then they traveled onward, piercing the walls of the makeshift hotel. The old structure, already weakened by time and weather, could take no further abuse. It collapsed in a dusty heap, burying fifty dying tenants beneath its crushing weight.

Chaney watched in his side-view mirror for the coup de grâce. It came a moment later. A glob of wired plastic explosive belched flame, splitting the steel reservoir of the water town in half. A cascade of water crashed down upon the collapsed barn, drenching the jagged timbers and whatever lay beneath it. The significance of that crowning touch was that the water was holy. Chaney had blessed it, using a prayer he had bought from a convent across the Mexican border, before he had set the timer and joined the others in line.

"Filthy bloodsuckers!" said Chaney as he headed for the open desert. He pushed a tape into the cassette player and rocked and rolled down the long abandoned highway toward the sweltering blur of the distant horizon.

.   .   .

"You sure you don't want something to drink?" the bartender asked Stoker, who sat alone at a corner table.

"No," replied the bearded man. "I'm fine."

"You sure? Beer, whiskey? Some wine, maybe?"

Stoker stifled a grin. "No, thank you."

The bartender shrugged and went about his business. The tavern, named Apocalypse After Dark, was empty except for Stoker and the barkeep. A wild-eyed fellow had been playing the slot machine an hour before, but the geek had left after his tokens were depleted. *Ghoul,* Stoker had thought to himself. *Probably rummaging through the death pyres right now, looking for warm leftovers.*

But Stoker had no interest in cannibals that night. At least not the kind that sneak around in shame, feeding off disposal plants and graveyards.

He sat there for another hour before he heard the sound that he had been waiting for. The sound of motorcycles roaring in from the west.

Headlights slashed across the front window of the saloon. Engines gunned, then sputtered into silence. Stoker tensed, wishing he had ordered that drink now. His hand went beneath the table, caressing the object he wore slung beneath his bomber jacket.

He watched them through the front window as they dismounted their Harley Davidsons like leather-clad cowboys swing from the saddles of chromed horses. There were an even dozen of them; eight men and four women. Another woman, naked, sat perched on the back of the leader's chopper. She was chained to the sissy bar, a dog collar around her slender throat keeping her from escaping.

"Poor angel," whispered Stoker. He was going to enjoy this immensely.

The batwing doors burst open and in they came. Bikers; big, hairy, ugly, and ear-piercingly loud. They wore studded leather with plenty of polished chains, zippers, and embroidered swastikas. On the back of their cycle jackets were their colors. A snarling wolf's head with flaming eyes and the words BLITZ WOLVEN.

"A round for me and the boys before we do our night's work," bellowed the leader, a bear of a man with matted red hair and beard. His name was Lycan. Stoker knew that from asking around. The names of the others were not important.

The bartender obediently filled their orders. Lycan took a big swig from his beer, foam hanging from his whiskers like the slaver of a rabid dog. He turned around and leaned against the bar rail, instantly seeing the man who sat alone in the shadowy corner. "How's it going, pal?" Lycan asked neighborly.

Stoker said nothing. He merely smiled and nodded in acknowledgement.

"How about a drink for my silent friend over yonder," the biker said. "You can put it on my tab."

The bartender glanced at the man in the corner, then back at Lycan. "Told me he didn't want nothing."

"What's the matter, stranger?" asked a skinny fellow with safety pins through each nostril. "You too good to drink with the likes of us?"

"I have a low tolerance for alcohol," Stoker said. "It makes me quite ill."

"Leave the dude alone," said Lycan. "Different strokes for different folks, I always say."

The skinny guy gave Stoker a look of contempt, then turned back to the bar.

"It takes all kinds to make a world," replied Stoker. "Especially a brave, new world such as this."

"Amen to that," laughed Lycan. He downed his beer and called for another.

"Blitz Woven? Does that have a hidden meaning? Are you werewolves or
Nazis?"

Lycan's good natured mood began to falter. He eyed the loner with sudden suspicion. "Maybe a little of both. So what's it to you?"

Stoker shrugged. "Just curious, that's all."

"Curiosity killed the cat," said an anorexic chick with a purple

Mohawk. "Or bat or rat... depending on what supernatural persuasion you are these days."

"I'll keep that in mind, dear lady."

"Well, enough of this bullshitting, you freaks," said Lycan. "Time to get down to business." They left the bar and walked to the far end of the tavern where a number of hooks jutted from the cheap paneling. Stoker watched with interest as they began to disrobe, hanging their riding leathers along the wall.

"What is this?" he asked. "The floor show?"

"You know, buddy," said Lycan, his muscular form beginning to contort and sprout coarse hair. "You're whetting my appetite something fierce. In fact, you might just be our opening course for tonight."

Stoker sat there, regarding them coolly. "I'm afraid not, old boy. I've got business of my own to attend to."

They were halfway through the change now. Faces distorted and bulged, sprouting toothy snouts and pointed ears. "Oh, and what would that be?" asked Lycan, almost beyond the ability to converse verbally. He stretched his long hairy arms, scraping the ceiling with razor claws.

Stoker stood up, stepped away from the table, and brought an Uzi submachine gun from under his jacket. "I'll leave that to your brutish imaginations," he said and opened fire.

The one with the pins in his nose began to howl, brandishing his immortality like some garish tattoo. Then he stopped his bestial laughter when he realized the bullets that were entering his body were not cast of ordinary lead. He screamed as a pattern of penetrating silver stitched across his broad chest, sending him back against the wall. He collapsed, smoking and shriveling, until he was only a heap of naked, gunshot man.

"Bastard!" snarled the female werewolf with the violet Mohawk. She surged forward, teeth gnashing, breasts bobbing and swaying like furry pendulums.

Stoker unleashed a three-round burst, obliterating the monster's head. It staggered shakily across the barroom, hands reaching up and feeling for a head, but only finding a smoking neck stump in its place. The werewolf finally slumped against the jukebox with such force that it began blasting out an old Warren Zevon tune with a boom of bass and tickling of ivory.

"How appropriate," said Stoker. He swept the barroom at a wide angle, holding the Uzi level with the ten remaining werewolves. One by one, they were speared by the substance they loathed the most. The beasts dropped to the saloon's sawdust floor, writhing and twitching in agony, before growing still.

Lycan leaped over the bar, ducking for cover as Stoker swung the machine gun in his direction. Slugs chewed up the woodwork, but nothing more. After a few more seconds of continuous fire, the Uzi's magazine gave out. Stocker shucked the clip and reached inside his jacket for a fresh one.

That was when Lycan, fully transformed now, sprang over the splintered bar top and tore across the tavern for his intended victim, smashing tables and chairs in his path. "You ain't gonna make it!" rasped Lycan. It came out more as a garbled snarl than an actual threat.

"Quite to the contrary," Stoker said calmly. He drew a serrated combat knife from his boot and thrust it upward just as Lycan came within reach. The sterling silver blade sank to the hilt beneath the werewolf's breastbone.

Lycan staggered backward, staring dumbly at the smoking knife in his

midsection. He looked at Stoker with bewildered eyes, then fell over stone cold dead, the impact of silver-shock shorting out his bestial brain cells.

Stoker walked over and withdrew the dagger from the wolf's body, wiping the blade on the fur of Lycan's vanishing coat. He slipped the weapon back into its sheath and looked toward the bartender, who was peeking over the edge of the bar. "How much do I owe you for damages?"

"No charge," the man said, pale-faced but happy. "I've been trying to keep this mangy riff-raff outta my joint for years."

Stoker left Apocalypse After Dark and stood outside for a long moment, enjoying the crisp night air and the pale circle of the full moon overhead. Then he noticed Lycan's pet sitting on the back of the Harley. He walked over to the girl and smiled at her softly. He cupped her chin in his hand. "Poor angel," he said soothingly, then blessed her with a kiss.

"What a glorious night, don't you think, my dear?" he asked as he swung aboard the big chopper and stamped on the starter, sending it roaring into life. The woman was silent, but she snuggled closer, wrapping her arms around his waist, and laying her weary head upon his shoulders.

Together, they winged their way into the dead of night.

Chaney parked his van between a black Trans-Am and a rusty Toyota pickup. He left his vehicle and mounted the steps of the Netherworld Café, a local hangout for the natural and unnatural alike.

He walked in and started down the aisle for the rear of the restaurant. A wispy ghost of a waitress took orders, while a couple of zombie fry-cooks slung hash behind the counter. Chaney waved to a few old acquaintances, then headed for the last booth on the right. Stoker was sitting there, poised and princely, as usual. There was a girl, too, wearing Stoker's bomber jacket and nothing else.

Chaney sat down and ordered the usual. Stoker did the same. They regarded each other in silence for a moment, then Chaney spoke up. "Well, is it done?"

"It is," nodded Stoker. "And what about you?"

"I kept my end of the bargain."

"Good," said Stoker. "Then it's settled. I get the blood."

"And I the flesh," replied Chaney.

They shook on their mutual partnership then, Chaney's hirsute hand emblazoned with the distinctive mark of the pentagram, while Stoker's possessed the cold and pale bloodlessness of the undead.

THE GENERAL'S ARM

LEE MOURNED.

Standing atop a wooded ridge in northern Virginia, he watched as an army train wound its way through the valley below, heading southward for Richmond. He had been present at the Spotsylvania depot a half hour before, watching solemnly as six Confederate soldiers hefted a pine casket from off a wagon bed and carried it to a waiting boxcar. Before the double doors of the car had been secured, the general had leaned forward, placed the palm of his hand against the wood, and prayed. When he had finished, his eyes had been moist with tears.

"Onward along the path to Glory, dear friend," he had rasped in scarcely a whisper. "My heart bleeds in loss... as does as our beloved Dixie."

Then the soldiers fastened the door latch securely. The locomotive had hissed and creaked, belching billows of coal smoke, anxious to be on its way. Unable to remain any longer, Robert E. Lee had turned, walked to a sugar maple nearby, and swung atop his iron gray gelding. Taking the reins from the grasp of an attending soldier, he swung Traveller's head eastward and sent him galloping up a narrow deer path toward the top of the ridge that he now stood on.

Although they had been victorious, the battle at Chancellorsville had taken a toll on the Army of Northern Virginia in more ways than one. Many a loyal soldier had fallen from mini-ball and bayonet, but the most loyal man under Lee's command had perished at the hands of his own men through a tragic case of mistaken identity.

Thomas "Stonewall" Jackson had been an astute military strategist and a respected commander of men, but he had also been General Lee's confidant and good friend. Both men were West Point graduates, seasoned generals, and devout men of faith. Lee and Jackson were brothers in Christ as well as brothers in arms. When a Confederate picket had mistakenly taken Jackson and his officers for Union cavalry on the Plank Road, their volley had killed several and severely wounded Stonewall. Three musket balls had shattered the bones of the lieutenant general's left arm, making amputation necessary. When Lee had heard of Jackson's physical loss, he had told an aide, "Jackson has lost his left arm, but I have lost my right."

The wounded general was taken to the Fairfield plantation for recovery, but he succumbed to pneumonia eight days later. His final words before his demise were, "Let us cross over the river and rest in the shade of the trees."

Now the man's body was in transport, heading to a hero's funeral, and Lee was without his finest commander. Morale among the soldiers was at its lowest point. The loss of Jackson had hit the troops and their superiors hard, but Lee was the hardest hit of all. Along with heartfelt grief, he also felt an awful sense of loss and doubt. As the army advanced northward toward West Virginia and Pennsylvania, he found his concentration taxed and his confidence shaken. J.E.B. Stuart and A.P. Hill were apt replacements, but they lacked the tenacity and boldness that Stonewall had possessed. Jackson had been the Confederacy's best chance at victory, and now that chance was beyond reach.

Or was it?

With a heavy heart, Lee removed his hat, revealing his thick shock of snow-white hair. He knelt, bowed his head, and, once again, prayed. "Lord Almighty, grant me forgiveness for what I am about to do. I know it is an atrocity in your eyes, but given the circumstances, I see no other course of action. I would gladly give my life to bring Tom Jackson back... but since that is impossible, I must resort to other, more unsavory methods. Bless my mission, if it be thy will. If not, damn me for my lack of faith and for what I now intend to accomplish."

Wearily, Lee stood, placed his hat upon his head, and swung back into the saddle. He ran a hand absently through Traveller's coal black mane, then reined the gelding back down the ridge toward the Confederate encampment below. Halfway along the grade, he realized he had not sealed his prayer with an "amen."

It was the first of many blasphemies to come.

The darkness of the spring evening had fallen across a dense wood near Ely's Ford on the Rappahannock River — a place the locals called the Wilderness — when General Lee strolled from campfire to campfire. The men of the encampment were surprised to see him out alone, without the accompaniment of his officers, and on foot. It was not odd that he was mingling among them; Lee was accessible and kind to his soldiers, not arrogant, like many generals in the field. They were simply unaccustomed to seeing him out after dark, drifting from one camp to another, his face as pale as bed linen and his eyes deeply troubled.

As the forest grew thicker, he approached a fire with three infantrymen huddled around it, supping on hardtack and jerked beef. "Could you gentlemen tell me where I could find Flinton Wells?" he asked, pausing before them.

The largest of the three, a burly man with muttonchop sideburns and a butternut uniform dyed by hand, regarded him grimly. "You oughtn't to be around him, General. You're a fine Christian man.

The boy is no-account... more of the devil than of God. I'd steer clear of the likes of him if'n I were you"

"That is my choice and mine alone, soldier," the commanding officer said, but with resignation and not anger. "Now tell me... where does he camp?"

The infantryman nodded over his shoulder to a lone fire flickering distantly in the darkness of the woods. "He billets on the bank of the river. I meant no offense, sir. Just concerned for your welfare is all. We can walk with you, if'n you'd like."

"No need for that, son." Lee's steely eyes gleamed in the light of the fire, regretful, as he stared off into the gloom of the trees. "There are some things a man must seek alone and this is one of them."

The general stepped high through the dense kudzu, picking his way through the dark bramble. Something about that section of the forest disturbed him, for he seemed to have wandered from the comfort of a thousand campfires into utter blackness. His ears strained for the chirp of crickets or the song of a whippoorwill, but neither could be heard. The silence was both complete and unsettling.

Nervously, he stroked his white beard. Lee felt as though he was being watched from a dozen different vantage points, by things that were neither human nor animal. Lee customarily wore no sidearm, but he had brought his Colt Walker with him that evening; the one he carried crossways in a scabbard from the pommel of Traveller's saddle. The big revolver was tucked securely in the belt of his tunic. He laid his right hand upon the walnut grip, but found no comfort in its presence. A .44 bullet would have no effect against things of an otherworldly nature, which was the impression he received as he trudged further into the depths of the dark thicket.

He heard the steady roar of the river. Moments later, he had reached the camp on the bank. He found a single man sitting upon a stone; tall and lanky, more bones than meat. He wore no uniform, only woolen britches, mule-ear boots, a hand-sewn shirt, and suspenders. The man held a branch over the flames of his fire.

Impaled upon the whittled end was a rat, skinned, but still possessing its head, tail, and appendages.

Lee was repulsed by the choice of supper, but he reckoned it was more nourishing than dried meat and hardtack. "Are you Flinton Wells?" he asked.

When the man lifted his head and revealed the face beneath the brim of his slouch hat, Lee discovered that he wasn't a man at all. He couldn't have been more than sixteen years of age. Still, it wasn't a fresh, child-like visage possessed by most of the young-sters who had fought and died in his ranks. The boy's gaunt face was sunken and horribly scarred. The disfigurement ran in a circular pattern, from the top of his forehead, along his cheeks and jawline, and then back again. A scrubby black mustache and goatee graced his upper lip and chin, and the pupils of his eyes were strangely pale, nearly to the point of whiteness, like ice upon a winter pond.

"I'm Flint," he answered and nodded to a fallen log on the oppo-site side of the fire. "Have yourself a seat, General."

Lee hesitated for a moment, knowing that he should be in his tent resting, instead of seeking help from the ungodly. He stepped over the log and sat down heavily, feeling as though his strength had left him. For the first time since the beginning of the War Between the States, Robert Lee felt every bit of his fifty-six years.

Flint studied the commanding officer and smiled. "I half expected you to come calling. You're a godly man, but the finest of Christians feel that their needs outweigh those of the Almighty every now and then."

"I don't feel that way at all, sir," proclaimed Lee haughtily.

Flint's pale eyes twinkled. "Is that so? Then why are you sitting here before my fire?"

The general sighed and his shoulders sagged an inch. "I've... I've heard tell that you can..."

"Bring the dead back to life?" Flint turned the rat in the flames until its tiny eyes sputtered and popped.

Lee nodded. "The soldiers claim that you have revived two

horses in the field. And a young child at Antietam who took a musket ball through his heart."

"Do you believe that I can do such things?"

"I once believed that only Lord Jesus could perform such miracles, but lately I have wondered if these tales of resurrection on the battlefield are true." The moment the words left his lips, Lee felt like Peter denying Christ at the third crow of the cock.

Flinton Wells removed his meal from the fire and yanked the rodent's hind leg from the moorings of its hip. He tore at the roasted flesh with his crooked teeth. "I am the seventh son of a seventh son," he said as he chewed. "Born of a woman at the instant of her death and wearing a veil of flesh upon my face. The doctor cut away the veil, but he could not strip me of what I was or of the things I was destined to do. In the olden days, they would have called me a sorcerer or conjurer. I don't rightly know what folks would call me these days... Lucifer's spawn, I suppose. Unless they have need of my services, that is." He tossed the tiny leg-bone into the fire and bit into the back of the rat, stripping the flesh from its spine. "So tell me, who is it that you want brought back to life?"

Lee said it, although his ears could scarcely believe the words. "General Jackson."

Flint chuckled. "Old Blue Light Jackson standing like a wall of stone." He considered it for a moment while he ate. "It could be done, except for one problem. The good general's remains are on their way to the governor's mansion in Richmond, to lie in state. That poses something of a dilemma."

"So you can do nothing without his body present?"

Flint scratched his bristly chin and stared into the fire, past the flames and into the glowing embers just beyond. "Now I didn't say that. There is one chance we can take."

"Go on. Speak your thoughts."

"Where is his arm?"

At first, Lee was unsure of what he referred to. "Arm?"

"The arm Jackson lost before his death," said Flint. "What became of it after the surgeon removed it? Was it discarded?"

"No. It was buried immediately afterward."

"Do you know where?"

Lee nodded. "Beneath an oak tree at Ellwood, the house of J. Horace Lacy in Orange County, near the field hospital. Jackson's chaplain interred it there."

"Then bring me the remains of the arm and I will have something to work with," Flint told him.

It would be a half day's ride there and back, but Lee felt that it was his only option. And he would not dare dispatch a courier to Orange County to do the job, either. He would retrieve the limb himself.

The General stood up. "I will see what I can do." He regarded the boy with distaste. "And what would you require for payment?"

Flint laughed loudly. "Payment? You mean like your mortal soul or your firstborn child? This is not a fairy tale, General. I work for the betterment of my clients and the satisfaction it provides. Just seeing Stonewall perched upon Little Sorrel once again, leading his troops into battle, will be worth much more than gold in my pockets."

Lee turned and left. As he carefully picked his way back through the forest, he heard Flinton Wells' laughter drift through the darkness. "Oh yea of little faith," he called contemptuously. "At least in the one you once held in such high regard."

After tossing on his cot for an hour, unable to sleep, Lee rose.

Opening the flap of his tent, he flipped open the lid of his pocket watch. The pale light of a half-moon showed the time to be 10:52. He stood there in indecision for a long moment, then knew what he must do. The general pulled on his riding boots, slipped on his tunic and sash, and left the tent, hat in hand.

Quietly, he saddled Traveller and fit the bit and bridle in place. He then took a shovel and a kerosene lantern from the bed of a supply wagon and secured them to the saddle. Looking southward, he swung atop the stone gray gelding and urged him along the dark road in the direction of Chancellorsville.

It took him two and a half precarious hours to reach the shadowy estate of Ellwood in Orange County. On his way, he had skirted two Union encampments, keeping enough distance so that the soldiers on guard couldn't detect him or that the horses picketed there wouldn't pick up Traveller's scent. Finally, Lee reached the outskirts of the plantation. Silently, he tied his horse's reigns to the upper beam of a split-rail fence. Then he took the lantern, the shovel, and a burlap bag, and climbed over the fence. Halfway across, a sharp sliver of wood sliced across the flat of Lee's palm, opening the flesh and drawing blood. The general's breath hissed between his teeth, but he uttered no further noise. He would worry about the wound after he had done what he came to do.

He kept low as he crossed a broad pasture and approached the dark outbuildings on the northern side of the Lacy property. The big white oak tree towered darkly on the far side of the smoke-house. Lee kept to the shadows and, soon, was crouched at the base of the trees. He found a mound of grassless earth between two knotted and exposed roots and knew that he had found the place where the amputated limb had been buried.

Lee lit the lantern and trimmed the wick until only a minimum amount of light shown, illuminating the patch of earth. Ignoring the laceration on his palm, he took the shovel in his hands and began to dig.

Stonewall's chaplain had buried the general's left arm deeply, to discourage stray dogs or raccoons from digging it up. Two feet down, he found it. It had been wrapped in bloody bed linen. Lee really did not want to cast eyes upon the severed appendage, but felt that it was necessary to ensure that it was precisely what he had come for. Carefully, in the light of the lamp, he unwrapped the cloth and stared at Jackson's amputated arm. It was bloated and as pale as baking flour, with blue veins running in dark relief against the bloodless flesh. The position of the thumb on the curled hand told him that it had, indeed, been taken from the left side. As he lifted the limb to place it within the tow sack, his fingers burst through the swollen bicep. A flood of dead maggots poured from the split in the dead muscle.

Lee closed his eyes and fought a wave of nausea that threatened to overcome him. *Are you mad?* he wondered. *Have you gone completely insane?*

He had stowed the offensive length of decaying flesh and bone away into the burlap bag and was cinching its mouth with twine, when someone spoke from directly behind him.

"Pardon me… but might I ask why you're out here, digging earth, in the dead of night?"

Startled, the commanding officer turned and confronted the one who stood no more than eight feet away. The orange glow of the lantern revealed a small, squat Negro woman of advanced years. She was dressed in a hand-sewn calico dress, a white apron around her ample hips, and a faded bandanna around the crown of her head. Her face was dark and deeply lined, like the head of an apple doll, skillfully carved and left in the sun to wither and shrink. Traces of dark hair laced with silver peeked from the corners of the bandanna, but her eyes were as clear and youthful as those of a child, although they also held a wisdom and rural savvy that was almost ancient in nature.

Before he could think of an answer, she spoke for him. "I know who you are, Robert Lee. What I don't know or understand is why you're out here well past midnight, digging up the lost arm of Stonewall Jackson?"

Lee swallowed dryly. "And, may I ask, why you are out here at the same lonesome hour? And how do you know that what I hold is what you claim it to be?"

The old woman smiled thinly. "To answer the first, I couldn't sleep. It's an ailment of mine… I scarcely get myself a wink or two of a night. And to answer your second question, it is indeed the general's arm, for I stood betwixt the smokehouse and the tool shed yonder and watched as the preacher man placed it in the hole and laid it to sod."

Lee knew there was no need to deny it any longer. "I'm digging it up so that it may be reunited with the rest of my friend's body. The chaplain buried it, believing that General Jackson would survive his unfortunate wounding. As you well know, that was not to be."

"If what you say be the truth, then fine and dandy," the old woman allowed. "But you know something peculiar about me? I can sense a bald-faced lie like a divining stick can lead you to water. And, right now, your words are ringing of a falsehood."

Lee straightened to his full height, his pale beard thrust forward. "Are you branding me a liar, madam?"

She laughed softly, dark eyes twinkling. "Now ain't that a hoot! I'd say you're the first white gentleman to treat me in such a respectful manner." The little woman's eyes suddenly lost their sparkle and grew as flat and gray as creek stones. "If you are deceiving me and have another use for that arm, I urge you to think better of it. The fate of the Confederacy is not so desperate that you should commit an abomination in the eyes of the Lord in an attempt to set things right. God does everything for a reason, General. Perhaps He took Ol' Stonewall in order to end this wicked war. In that case, you ought to stick that rotten piece of meat back in the earth and cover it over."

"I can't do that," Lee said. The lie he spoke lay across his tongue — and his heart — with the weight of a millstone. "I promised his dear wife that I would retrieve his arm so that his remains could be wholly committed to the grave."

"Very well," said the old woman. "But if it be otherwise, may the good Lord have mercy on your soul... as well on the rest of this poor, battle-scarred nation."

The statement disturbed him. "What do you mean by that?'

"If you be truthful, you may never know. But if you're not, you shall find out soon enough."

As Lee picked up the shovel, he grimaced in pain.

"You're hurt," the woman said, concerned. "Let me take a look-see."

"You need not concern yourself..."

"Hush," she scolded, "and give me your hand."

Lee watched as she examined the laceration and then dipped a dark-skinned hand into the pocket of her apron. She brought forth a small jar and uncapped it. Gently coating the wound with a pale salve that smelled of sulfur and honeysuckle, the old woman then released him.

"There, that oughta do you."

He watched as she turned and started back across the shadowy yard, to where a row of small tin and tarpaper shanties stood at a distance from the main house. "Might I ask, what exactly is your name, good lady?"

She turned and smiled over her humped shoulder. "They call me the Granny Woman. If I ever had a name other than that, I reckon it was cast away and forgotten long ago."

"I'm obliged to you," he said sincerely.

"The salve and advice was free," she told him curtly. "And so is further help, if ever you should need it, Robert E. Lee. If that day comes, you know where to find me."

Then she stepped between the darkness of two storage sheds and was gone from sight. General Lee stared down at the thing in his hands and considered chucking it back into the hole from where it had been liberated. But his grief and his desperation were blinding and, instead, he tied it securely to the horn of the saddle's pommel, despite the skittishness of Old Traveller.

He journeyed the remainder of that night, contemplating his purpose for the nocturnal ride, as well as his unexpected meeting with the old Negro woman.

When the first rays of dawn lit his path, he looked down at the palm of his hand and found that the flesh had closed in upon itself and was completely healed.

The Army of Northern Virginia remained encamped in the wooded wilderness beside the Rappahannock River for the next few days. Many had been injured during the bloody battle at Chancellorsville and those who had not suffered from bayonet or bullet were physically exhausted. The troops' morale was at rock bottom, too; the worst Lee had seen since the beginning of the war.

And, following the commander's return from Orange County, there was deep-seated fear and apprehension as well.

After Lee had arrived back at the encampment, Flinton Wells requested that a tent be erected several hundred yards from the camp, with nothing but a single canvas cot placed within. After his instructions were fulfilled, the boy took a knapsack of essentials he would need and the burlap bag and went inside. He stayed there for two days and two nights. At first he was alone, but as the hours passed, it was clear to those in the camp that his solitude had come to an end and that someone — or *something* — was within the shelter, keeping company with him.

The soldiers became restless and suspicious of the goings-on in the lone tent, and with good reason. Even from where they camped, they could hear the boy chanting in an unknown tongue, his voice alternating from hushed whispers to lungful shouts. And his were not the only sounds that came from beyond the closed flaps of the tent. At night, they heard unnerving noises that they could neither identify as animal or human. Low whimpers of torment, sobbing, laughter, and, even once or twice, shrill screams of agony that would cause the short hairs on the back of a man's neck to stand on end.

As dissention among the soldiers steadily grew, Lee felt compelled to walk among the ranks and offer reassurance. "Let patience be your virtue," he would tell them. "Put your faith in the Lord and all of this will become known. Believe me, it will be well worth the wait."

Even as he spoke those appeasing words, the general felt like the worst of hypocrites. He knew better than any of them that what was going on in the tent was not anything sanctioned by the will or might of God, or anything of an earthly realm either. As Flint's strange chanting grew louder and more urgent, it was clear to Lee, and anyone within earshot, that whatever miracle was being performed in the bailiwick, it had more to do with Lucifer than of Jehovah. He began to wish that he had heeded the soldier's warning, abandoned his search for the teen-aged conjuror, and simply walked away.

But his hopes for a Southern victory and, perhaps, personal pride on his own part, caused him to allow the hidden ritual to continue, despite his misgivings. He knew that his decision to do so was a blasphemy against his God and his faith, but he could not bear to see those he commanded suffer needless death and maiming injury any longer. If he didn't proceed with his original intentions, they would likely end up in an unmarked grave on some cannon-blown battlefield or confined in a disease-infested prison camp such as Douglas or Elmira.

During the first night of Flint's isolation, Lee's curiosity got the better of him. Shortly after midnight, he crossed the pasture and made his way toward the tent. The canvas walls of the structure were lit with a flickering glow from within. At first, the light seemed normal; pale and orange. Then it intensified, alternating between blood red, deep cobalt blue, and then ebbed back to flickering orange again.

Lee paused. Then, unannounced, drew the flap aside.

What he witnessed rattled him to the very depths of his soul.

Flint sat cross-legged on the floor of the tent, next to the army cot. Stubby candles of black tallow were positioned in a sweeping oval around him. As he chanted, his face was deathly pale while the ring of scar tissue that wreathed his countenance was red and inflamed. His eyes had rolled back into the sockets of his skull until only the whites could be seen. It looked to Lee as though the boy was in the throes of some sort of trance.

But, as if Flint's condition wasn't startling enough, the thing lying upon the cradle of wood and canvas was even more disturbing.

At first glance, it appeared that someone had skinned a large dog and left its bleeding carcass on the cot. But as Lee studied the writhing bundle of raw muscle and denuded tendons, he abruptly realized that it was the upper torso and head of a *man*... or something that was gradually becoming one.

The fleshless mass seemed to sprout from the left arm Lee had dug from the earth at the base of the white oak tree. The limb was no longer pale and subject to rigor mortis. The flesh was now vibrant and healthy, and the hand flexed involuntarily, the tendons working like lean cords beneath the skin. Lee turned his eyes upon the head, which strained upward on the column of its neck. It was fleshless and devoid of hair, yet he could tell by its very profile precisely who it was.

"Jackson!" Lee exclaimed in both awe and horror.

At the name, the thing sluggishly turned its head and stared in his direction with blind, white eyes.

"It is not yet time, General," scolded Flint. His pupils were aligned once again, irritated at the interruption.

"How long will it be until this cursed process comes to fruition?" Lee demanded.

"I am not God," Flint told him flatly. "I cannot take soil in hand and breathe life into it. What you asked for will come to pass soon enough. Now depart and leave me to my business."

Lee turned his attention to the mass of raw muscle and sinew that twisted and lurched on the blood-drenched cot. It turned its head toward the door of the tent once again, blew sanguine bubbles from its nostrils, and smiled.

"My friend," it gurgled, or so it seemed in Lee's ears. The Confederate commander quickly turned and left that place with a fervent prayer upon his lips.

A prayer, he feared, that fell upon unreceptive ears because of his arrogance and self-serving ways.

Early on the morning of May 10th, 1863, the collective ranks of Lee's Army of Northern Virginia assembled in the pasture around the lone tent. An air of mistrust and grudging curiosity hung about the soldiers as they waited expectantly in the dewy grass of the field.

Lee's officers, as well as Generals Hood and Stuart, encircled the tent, facing their troops, their backs against the canvas walls. Their commander had instructed them to do so, stating, "We must maintain order at the very moment that this miracle is revealed. What the reaction of these men shall be, I have no idea. It could be jubilation or mutiny. Your guess as to which is as good as mine."

The general stood before the flaps of the tent, holding a bundle of clothing and a pair of polished riding boots in his hands. Outwardly, he seemed poised and unaffected, but inwardly he was gripped by a mixture of anxiousness and dread. He thought of the awful thing that had lain writhing, half-formed, on the bloody cot and something the old Negro woman at Ellwood had said came back to him. *An abomination in the eyes of the Lord*, the Granny Woman had called it, referring to Lee's acquisition of the buried arm. Initially, Lee had been certain that she hadn't an inkling of what his true intentions for it had been. Or had she, in her own way, secretly known precisely what he had been up to?

At the hour of seven, the flaps opened inward and Flint Wells stood in the entranceway. "Come in, General, and see what my handiwork has brought about."

Lee stepped inside the tent, and instantly his breath caught in his throat, refusing to expel. There, before him, as naked as in birth, stood Thomas Jonathan Jackson. The man was his friend and comrade in all physical ways; medium of stature, lean of frame, with dark, receding hair and a thick beard and mustache upon his gaunt face. The dark gray eyes sparkled with recognition the moment they regarded him, and he extended his right hand in welcome.

"Bob," he said in Stonewall's undeniable voice. "Dammit, it is good to see you again, my friend."

Lee felt so overwhelmed by the man's resurrection that dizziness and disorientation nearly gripped him for a second. Then, steeling his nerve, he took a couple of steps forward and halted, averting his eyes. "Cloth yourself, Tom, and we shall embrace as brothers do."

The man laughed heartily. "Ever the prude!" he declared and dressed himself. Stonewall had been a humble man in his former life. He had never gone for the dress uniforms that Lee and most of his fellow generals preferred, instead wearing threadbare clothing in the field and a pair of scuffed boots that had been repaired by the cobbler many times over the years. As he adjusted the sash of his tunic and pulled on the boots, he nodded in approval. "Befitting a true champion of the Cause," he said boldly.

Lee regarded the man sagely. The smile on his face managed to conceal the doubt that was gradually creeping upon him. In many ways, the man who stood before him was identical to the one he had known for years, while in other, very important ways, he was the complete opposite. His swearing and his vanity were uncharacteristic of the devout Presbyterian that Lee had served with during the duration of the War Between the States. But he said nothing to challenge such noticeable differences.

As Jackson stood, Lee stepped forward and embraced him as he had promised. Beyond the uniform, he felt a great heat radiate from the man's body, as though he were in the throes of a high fever. He leaned forward, bringing his lips near his friend's ear. "How was the shade of the trees at the far side of the river?" he asked, remembering the last words the general had spoken before his passing.

"Not nearly as cool as I would have imagined," Jackson whispered back with a low chuckle.

The two parted. Lee stared into Jackson's face, trying hard to see someone other than his old friend. He saw nothing that said that the man who stood before him was otherwise. From all outward appearances, the bearded gentleman clad in Confederate gray was, indeed, Stonewall Jackson. It was just his behavior that had made him seem alien to Lee during the first few minutes of their reunion. Perhaps, during the miraculous incarnation of the general, he had returned with little memory of the honorable man and devout Christian that he had once been. It was a lapse that Lee hoped to alleviate in time as they grew reacquainted with one another.

"Are you prepared to face your men?" Lee asked him.

"Face them?" Jackson seemed amused. "You talk as though I am about to stand before a firing squad."

The commander knew that what he said might not be so far from the truth. "Tom... you were brought back to us by unnatural means. I understand what was involved – not all of it, but most – but they don't. I believe they are more frightened of seeing what emerges from this tent than you might think. And fear can bring about violence and retribution more swiftly than a match can light fire to dry tender."

"Then let us go out and assure them that there is nothing to fear," Jackson told him, sounding like the man who had led charges at Bull Run, Mechanicsville, and Sharpsburg.

A moment later, General Lee stepped through the flaps of the tent and confronted the troops who were assembled before them. Their faces were full of apprehension and mistrust. Their eyes shifted from Lee to the opening of the tent and then back again. It was obvious that their emotions had been primed by days of uncertainty and was as volatile and treacherous as a powder keg on the verge of detonation.

"I know that you have wondered what has been taking place here during the past two days," Lee told them, standing ramrod straight, his right hand perched upon the pommel of his saber. "Well, your uncertainty ends here and now." He stepped aside, clearing the entrance of the tent for what was to come. Lee's heart thundered in his chest as he watched the multitude of men that stood expectantly before him.

Then the flaps of the tent were swept aside, and Jackson emerged. A collective gasp rose from the throats of the troops and their eyes widened with bewilderment and disbelief. Some of them mouthed silent prayers, while others simply stared, dumbfounded, at the bearded man who stepped abruptly into view.

For a long moment, silence hung in the air like a palpable wall. Then Jackson spoke. "The news of my demise was vastly premature, gentlemen," he said in that crisp, Virginia drawl known by all who he had commanded over the years. "I have returned... to lead us all unto victory!"

There was a moment more of tense silence. Then, as one, a great roar of jubilation rose skyward. Depression and doubt were forgotten, and in their place, there was only relief and boundless wonder.

Jackson smiled, turned his head toward Lee, and winked. "I told you that there was nothing to fear, old friend."

Robert E. Lee attempted to take the man's words as the gospel truth, but found himself unable to do so. If anything, the general felt even more afraid than he had before. As though a dark and impenetrable darkness had emerged from the depths of Flint Wells' tent and circled, like a flock of buzzards, over the heads of the Army of Northern Virginia.

In the gathering gloom of a summer dusk, Lee kept well behind the one ahead of him, stealthfully following.

The past month had been a victorious one for the Confederate Army, but one that brought shame and misgivings upon the rebel commander. Numerous skirmishes, as well as the battle at Brandy Station, had been won at the merciless prodding of Stonewall Jackson... or the thing that masqueraded as him.

The sudden resurrection of Jackson had lifted the morale of every soldier and fortified them as a formidable fighting force. But that alone had not satisfied Stonewall. He drove his command past the boundaries of honor, into depths of cruelty and relentless bloodletting. This new incarnation of Jackson held a vindictiveness that the old one had never possessed. In a recent skirmish, Lee had watched as Stonewall commanded an infantry soldier to bayonet a wounded Union cavalryman. When the young soldier had refused, the general had leapt down off his horse, nearly decapitated the Yankee with his saber, and then turned and laid the blade across the rebel shoulder's cheek, leaving a scar that would mark him until his dying day. That had only been one of the disturbing actions displayed by the darker version of the Confederate general which Flint Wells' black magic had brought about.

And there were other things, as well. The Thomas Jackson that Lee had served with had been a devoted man of God and had read his Bible voraciously. Lee had loaned the man his own personal Bible several days ago, hoping that the reading of scripture might cause the general to realize the sort of man he had once been. Lee had found the burnt remains of the book in the ashes of a campfire the next evening.

And, strangely, the man never seemed to eat. At the daily meals, Stonewall Jackson was conspicuously absent. At the supper hour, he would mount Little Sorrell and head off into the woods, only to return a little past twilight.

That evening, Lee followed at a distance.

He watched from the shadows as Stonewall made his way through a grove of Virginia pines, coming upon a broad clearing. There, nibbling upon a bed of clover, was a young doe. At the sound of Jackson's horse drawing near, the deer raised her head. She stood frozen as the general raised his left hand, fingers splayed. The gesture had an unsettling effect on the animal. The doe's large eyes grew glazed and it dropped to its knees, almost as in submission to the man before it.

Jackson left his saddle and planted his feet on solid ground. A smile unlike any that had ever crossed the countenance of the true man, distorted the imposter's lips as he calmly walked forward. Lee watched uneasily as Jackson drew a bone-handled knife from his sash and drew the honed blade across the creature's throat. The steel blade parted flesh and hide and sank deeply. He could hear the rasp of the blade's edge grate against the hardness of the doe's vertebrae.

When the deer dropped to the carpet of clover, Stonewall sank to his knees, his eyes feverish and a bestial growl rumbling down deep in his throat. Then he took the animal in his hands and began to feast.

It was not the nourishment of a civilized man, but of something beyond that of humankind. Jackson's head dipped again and again, his teeth tearing, ripping, consuming at an errant pace. The noises that accompanied his eating were those of a wild dog, on the point of starvation and relentless, rather than those of a man.

Lee watched in horror. *Forgive me, Lord,* he prayed silently, *forgive me for what I have done.*

In the clearing, Jackson laughed softly. He turned his head, meat and blood matting his dark beard, and his eyes looked past the gloom, directly at his mentor. "Come," he called to him. "Sup with me."

Lee neglected to leave the shadows, but he spoke. "What manner of creature are you?"

"The same that I have been for ages, only now in the shell of a man you once loved and admired." Stringy bit of raw tissue hung between his teeth as he grinned. "Have you lost your devotion to Jackson, as you obviously have for your beloved Creator?"

The thing's words wounded Lee like a well-aimed bullet. "No, I still cherish both. It is you that I despise."

"You should embrace what you have brought about. The wheels have been set in motion. There is no ending it now."

Lee's spirits sank. In his heart, he believed that Jackson was correct in his boast. "I will decommission you. Take away your command."

Jackson eyed the general with contempt. "I obey a different superior,

Lee. You hold no authority over me or my methods."

Discouraged, Lee stepped back into the woods, intending to leave the fiend to its ravenous indulgence.

"We march for Pennsylvania soon," Stonewall told him. "I am afraid that I find my troops, shall we say, *lacking* in conviction and the desire for victory. We must do something to remedy that."

Quickly, Lee made it to where his horse was tethered. He climbed atop Traveller and made his way back through the forest toward camp. Behind him, he could hear the rending of flesh and the breaking of bones for the warm marrow within.

Later, after the encampment had settled in for the night, Lee sent for his best scout.

The man's name was Lowhorn, but he was known throughout the ranks of the Army of Northern Virginia as the Grey Ghost. Half white and half Cherokee Indian, Lowhorn was a master at reconnaissance and topography, and many of the maps he had devised of enemy brigades and their precise locations had won them many a battle in the past. He had earned his mysterious nomenclature from his ability to move through hostile territories undetected and infiltrate Union camps like a wraith. His horse, a black gelding named Midnight, was as stealthful and fleet of foot as his master. It was said that the steed had once silently killed a ten-foot rattlesnake in its path, no more than twenty feet from a heavily fortified Yankee picket, without the soldiers being any the wiser.

Lee finished penning a letter, sealed the flap, and handed it to the scout. "You must go to Ellwood in Orange County and hand this missive to Mr. Lacy personally. You will be returning with an old Negro woman whose help I have great need of. Her name is…"

"The Granny Woman," finished Lowhorn. "Yes, I know of her."

"Then you probably know *why* I am bringing her here."

The scout's dark eyes darkened even more. "I simply hope that we are not too late in fetching her."

Lee clamped an assuring hand on the man's shoulder. "That may depend solely on the speed with which you bring her, son."

Lowhorn nodded curtly. "I will deliver her to you safely, General."

Then he turned and, like a specter, vanished through the flaps of Lee's tent.

The most treasured military leader of the Confederate Army reclined heavily upon his cot, his forearm laid across his eyes. Despair threatened to overcome him, but he fought it down. He thought of the thing – the demon – who occupied the shelter a few tents away from him and saw his blood-spattered face in his mind, leering, taunting him with the weight of his shortcomings. He wondered if news of Stonewall's continued command had reached the ears of the Southern folk back home and how they would react to learning that the man they edified in memorial was still among the living... so to speak.

A deep drowsiness overtook him, and soon, he had drifted into a black and dreamless sleep.

He was awakened by a stern hand upon his arm.

"Rise, General," said the voice of Ambrose P. Hill. "There is something taking place in the pasture on the far side of the ridge."

"What is it?" he asked, startled. "What is happening?"

He saw another dark form directly behind the first; J.E.B. Stuart. "Jackson has assembled the troops there. How he did so without our knowledge, I have no idea. We must have slept heavily."

"We did," said Lee, pulling on his boots. "But not of our own accord. I believe that we were bewitched." When the commander was fully dressed, the three departed the tent and went for their horses.

Minutes later, they crouched at the top of the wooded ridge and stared at the vast, moonlit expanse of the pastureland below. Everyone was there; infantry, artillery, and cavalry. The gathering included the liverymen, the cooks, and the fife and drum boys as well. They all stood at attention, facing north-westward, in the direction of the border that divided Virginia from Maryland, and, beyond that, Pennsylvania.

Ahead of them was Stonewall Jackson atop Little Sorrel; ramrod straight and full of arrogance. In front of him was Flinton Wells. The boy was walking back and forth, from one side of the pasture to the other. His hand would dip into the pocket of a shoulder bag, grasp a fistful of something, and then scatter it across the earth.

"What in tarnation is that young'un doing?" asked Hill.

"Reminds me of Lucifer in the book of Job," grunted Stewart. "Walking up and down, to and fro."

Lee took a brass telescope from a sheath on his sash and unfolded it. He held it steady as he examined Flint and his peculiar actions. "He seems to be spreading something on the ground. A red dust of some sort."

When Flint had finally reached the far end of the pasture, Jackson nodded approvingly to the boy and then drew his saber. "Forward march!" he commanded.

The disgruntled soldiers hesitated at first. Then, wishing to get the exercise over with and return to their bedrolls, they started forward. They marched a hundred feet, their commander a fair distance ahead of them. Then something peculiar happened. Their feet, clad in scuffed boots and ragged footwear, began to churn up the crimson dust beneath them. It rose into the night air, almost like a mist, obscuring their lower extremities, from hip to toe.

"What's happening now?" asked Stewart. His bearded face was stern as he watched, with the naked eye, from the tree line atop the ridge.

Lee, on the other hand, had a better vantage point due to his telescope. His heart thudded in his chest as a muted red glow formed deep down in the mist at ground level. Then it brightened and grew with intensity. The red dust settled quickly, and the earth began to shift and crack beneath the feet of the Army of Northern Virginia. The men reacted with alarm as the fissures in the grassy mantle widened and flames burst explosively from the depths within.

The general's shock soon turned to horror as he witnessed a spectacle that was nearly beyond his comprehension. From the fiery bowels of the earth, long root-like tentacles of a wet blackness like that of fresh tar sprouted and entwined around the legs and torsos of the Confederate soldiers. The men screamed and fought frantically in their attempt to escape, but there seemed to be no way to conquer the things that had entrapped them. Bowie knives and bayonets merely glanced off the armored hardness of the tentacles with no visible effect. Then their terror increased as they were drawn, wailing and struggling, into the pasture's open cracks.

"The substance of nightmares," Lee muttered, finally answering Stuart's question. "That is what is taking place down there."

For a long moment, the field grew silent, except for the crackle of flames and the nervous shying of Little Sorrel. Lee shifted his spyglass to Jackson. Stonewall sat atop his horse, his eyes satisfied and a wicked grin upon his bearded face. Then something began to happen again, and Lee turned his attention back to the network of fissures that crisscrossed the open field. Things began to emerge from the fiery gorges; things that, for all outward appearances, looked like the men who had been swallowed up moments before. But the general knew that was far from being the case. Even from a distance, he could detect the grayness of their flesh and the unnatural glowing of their eyes, radiating from the shadows of their brows like the embers of a fire. Their movements were shaky and disjointed at first, then grew in fluidity and strength. Their uniforms, which had once been rebel gray or butternut beige, were now coal black and steaming with heat. As, one by one, they burst from the earth, a northern wind blew across the field, sending the stench of sulfur and decay drifting southward. When it reached the nostrils of the three Confederate generals, they retched, nearly to the point of vomiting.

"What madness is this?" demanded Hill, covering his lower face with the crook of his arm.

"It is raw, unbridled evil, Ambrose," Lee replied, his voice choked with despair. "And I am the sole cause of its coming."

Silently, the three watched as Jackson brandished his saber and motioned the unholy troops, several thousand strong, to follow. They did as they were directed, holding their weapons with a deliberation and single-mindedness that was downright disturbing to witness.

Soon, they had crossed the dark acreage and disappeared into the

forest beyond. Heading north, toward western Maryland... and the sovereign state of Pennsylvania beyond.

"Fall back," he said with caution. "We must not let them know they are being followed."

At the request of Robert E. Lee, generals A.P. Hill and J.E.B. Stewart reined their horses in, switching from a gingerly pace to a slow canter.

After the departure of Stonewall Jackson and his hellish army, the trio of commanders had returned to the encampment. They had hurriedly gathered

supplies, guns, and ammunition, and set off in pursuit.

For two days they rode, discovering new and unspeakable atrocities with each and every mile they gained. A farmstead with a burntout house and a barn with the skins of a man, woman, and three small children nailed to the weathered boards, their denuded and gnawed bones lying in a heap nearby. A traveling preacher crucified upon the boughs of an oak tree, his wrists and feet fastened to the wood with railroad spikes, his gaping mouth filled with pages of scripture from his defiled Bible, his eyes gouged out and lying in the dust of the road. And, worse of all, an entire village slaughtered without hesitation, the heads of the unfortunate citizens impaled upon the sixty-nine pickets of a graveyard fence, while within, graves had been unearthed and their remains abused and strewn about. Close by, Lee had seen a cornhusk doll speckled with blood, a tiny hand severed at the wrist still clutching it in death as it had in life.

By dusk, the three had seen a wanton disregard for human existence worse than anything performed upon the battlefield. They set up camp in a grassy clearing amid a stand of chestnut trees. Silently, they tethered their mounts and built a small fire. They ate sparingly, their stomachs weakened by the degradation they had witnessed, then settled in for the night. Despite the heaviness of their thoughts, it wasn't long before sleep claimed them.

It was in the dark, cool hours of early morning when Lee lurched from his slumber, aware that someone stood directly above him. He was startled

to see Stonewall Jackson – or the thing that had replaced him – staring down at him, his lean face ruddy with firelight.

When Lee looked to his fellow commanders, he found them still in the throes of a deep sleep. "They are of no consequence," Jackson told him. "It is you I have come to see."

"To put an end to me, I suppose," Lee said. "As you have a hundred
innocent folks who have crossed paths with you and your hell spawn."

"Not necessarily," the bearded man replied. "You are a clever and invaluable man, Robert Lee. You have turned your back on God. Now it is time that you bow to a new master and endure a baptism of brimstone."

"Never! I would rather kneel at the throne of the Almighty and be branded an infidel than to surrender my soul to the Devil!"

Jackson shrugged his narrow shoulders. "You shall do one or the other, eventually. It is up to you which path you choose." An expression that was almost compassionate and pleading crossed the general's countenance. "I would find no pleasure in killing you, Bob. Together, we can ride into victory once again. Cut a swath of destruction through Pennsylvania and Maryland and march down the streets of Washington. We shall conquer those who once opposed us, raping and profane all that they once cherished and held dear. And we shall burst through the doors of that alabaster palace and feast upon the heart of Lincoln himself!"

"And I hazard to guess that it would not end there, would it?" Lee countered with disgust. "Where would you venture after Washington is but a charred memory? Philadelphia, Boston, New York? Perhaps even London or Paris eventually?"

"There is much territory to conquer," Jackson admitted with a broad
smile. His teeth were longer and sharper than they had been mere seconds before. "With your assistance, we shall possess the world."

"If that is your goal, then you will achieve it without my help,"

Lee declared. "Now begone, fiend! I wish to look upon you no longer!"

"Very well," said the faux general. "But, rest assured, your days are numbered, Virginian. If you choose to stand against me and my kind, you will soon stand no more."

"Then so be it!"

Jackson laughed and, stepping beyond the reach of the fire's low glowing embers, vanishing from sight.

Lee sat amid his bedroll and breathed deeply, his heart pounding in distress.

"Calm yourself, Robert Lee," spoke a familiar voice. "Your days upon this earth are still plentiful and blessed."

The general turned his head sharply. The Granny Woman sat on a gray mule at the edge of the chestnut grove, the light of the campfire gleaming across her ebony face. Behind her, astride Midnight, was Lowhorn, the half-breed known as the Grey Ghost.

"Did you see him?" Lee wanted to know. "Or did he merely come to me in a dream?"

The old woman smiled gently, but her eyes were as hard and as cold as pig iron. "Oh, he was here, alright. Just as bold and full of piss and vinegar as Ol' Scratch his own self." Her expression changed and an instant later, the wrinkled flesh deepening, laden with equal parts of wisdom and mischievousness. "But he is not as invincible as he would hope to believe. It is time to make amends with the good Lord, don the armor and shield, and put an end to this sorry and sordid situation."

The following day, the four Confederates and the elderly woman rode

hard. The Granny Woman advised them to find a way around and ahead of Jackson and his exodus of depravity, for she claimed that confronting them face-to-face was the only way to defeat them.

Lowhorn knew the land well and soon figured out a route that would take them to their intended destination before nightfall.

While the army traveled through steep foothills and forged the Monocacy River at its shallowest point, the five riders circled north-eastward. Near the town of Elkins, they crossed a railroad trestle over the waterway, which put them a good three miles ahead of Jackson and his men. Spanning the bridge was treacherous for those on horseback, however. The lumber ties were spaced twelve inches apart and one misplaced hoof would have sent both mount and rider off balance and plunging two hundred feet into the rock-scattered current below. Luckily, the horses that carried the scout and generals were battle-seasoned and sure-footed, and so had no difficulty making the journey. The Granny Woman's sway-backed mule — who she rode side-saddle and called Nellie Mae — was as sturdy and trail savvy as the military steeds and, before long, they were back upon solid ground and at a full gallop.

As twilight fell, they camped atop a small hill thick with sycamore and fir. Even as they dined on a cold supper of dried pork and hardtack, they saw the glow of a small town aflame and heard distant screams. The terror and agony of the cries were such that the horses milled restlessly and their riders sat quietly in the darkness, their spirits heavy.

"We must end this travesty," Lowhorn said, as he downed a swallow of tepid water from a canteen. "It travels like wildfire in the dry of summer and devours all in its wake like a cancer."

"You three will stay here," the Granny Woman told him. She stood up

and stretched. The ancient bones of her spine popped and creaked. "Me and General Lee will ride down to the valley yonder. He will face the one who slanders the name of Stonewall Jackson with his dark deeds, while I shall take care of the rest."

The men stared at her as though she was mad, but said nothing to dissuade her. From the short time they had spent in her company, they knew that she was special in ways they could scarcely imagine. Where the hell-birthed Jackson was the very embodiment of evil, the Granny Woman possessed an equal share of goodness and grace.

As the two left the others behind, Lee atop Traveller and the

Granny Woman astride Nellie Mae, they were quiet as they made their way cautiously down the southern face of the hill. Both understood the magnitude of what was about to take place and the consequences for them — and perhaps all mankind — if they should fail at their mission.

Halfway there, Lee spoke aloud. "May I ask you something?"

"Go right ahead," the old lady replied.

"Do you think that I will burn in the lake of fire for what I have brought about?"

The Granny Woman chuckled softly. "I believe no such thing, Robert Lee. You are a good and kind-hearted man. Not a saint, but a man. The Lord may reprimand his children, but he will never forsake them."

"Not even for unlocking the gates of Hell and allowing the dregs of the pit to roam upon the earth?"

"It is natural for one who loves and cherishes to wish the dead back to life," she explained. "Most consider it for a fleeting moment, then pass it by. You acted upon the want because the possibility of doing so seemed beneficial to your people and their misguided cause. Mistakes are laden with good intentions, General, and, unfortunately, yours was of a generous portion."

"But how am I to conquer him? I am just a mortal man, while he commands the very demons of purgatory!"

The Granny Woman's dark eyes twinkled. "By taking back that which you first gave him."

Lee marveled at the old Negro's wisdom. "Might I ask... exactly how old you are?"

"I don't rightly remember," she told him truthfully. "I stopped counting a long time ago."

Then the ground beneath them leveled out, and they found themselves at the mouth of a narrow valley. Ahead of them, they could hear the thunderous rhythm of marching feet and the triumphant voice of their leader, urging them onward.

The Granny Woman slid down off her mule and took a sling sack from the provisions lashed to the animal's lower back. "Keep your nerve and we will sleep easy this night. Do you understand what you must do?"

Lee smiled and ran his right hand across the handle of his saber. "Yes, ma'am. I believe that I do."

"Then ride out to meet the bastard, and I will attend to the others."

The general watched as she dipped her dark hand into the belly of the sling sack and brought out a fistful of ebony pellets. "What are those?"

"Hell seed," she told him. "And when I sow it upon the ground, pay no mind to what takes place around you. Just put your heart and soul into laying the imposter low and you will not be harmed."

Lee nodded and looked to the far end of the valley. There in the grassy expanse between two towering cliffs, rode Jackson upon the horse who loathed him. Behind him crowded his dark troops, their eyes glowing like foxfire and their teeth matted with blood still warm to the touch.

"Take me into battle, Traveller," he requested, spurring the gelding on. The iron gray horse did not hesitate. It powered into a fluid gallop, nostrils flaring and head lowering like that of a charging bull.

Seeing his adversary approaching, Stonewall Jackson laughed and urged his own horse forward. Little Sorrel quickened his pace and soon matched Traveller's speed. Jackson drew his sword and brandished it overhead. Lee did the same. Clutching the gelding's reigns in one hand, he slid the honed blade of his saber from its scabbard with the other and rode onward.

The Granny Woman watched as Jackson's minions grasped their weapons and surged forward. The unnerving noise known as the "rebel yell" had never held as much fury and intimidation as it did at that moment. But the old woman did not falter. "Back to where you came, hellions!" she spat contemptuously. Then she took a fistful of the tiny, black seeds and cast them upon the earth ahead of her.

Instantly, the grass caught flame. But it was not the flickering orange-yellow of earthly fire, but the blue-white glow of heavenly lightning. The azure blaze swiftly surged forward, heading to meet those who came for her. A moment later, the blue fire reached Jackson's infernal troops and engulfed them. They wailed and shrieked as the earth beneath their feet opened and the dark tentacles that had once lifted them now dragged them downward once again.

At the same instant, Lee and Jackson met, furiously and without restraint. Swords clashed with such force that sparks glanced off the curved blades. Jackson laughed and reined his horse into a sweeping turn, then parried with his steel. The edge bit deeply into Lee's bearded cheek, drawing blood.

"Do you actually believe that you can defeat me?" he thundered, his voice multiplied like that of a hundred tortured souls. "Your black witch has conquered my ranks, but I am much harder to vanquish. I have existed since the beginning of time, Lee. And now that I have taken on a form of flesh and bone, I refuse to relinquish it!"

Robert E. Lee sent Traveller into a backward canter, avoiding an attack that would have surely decapitated him. He considered the Granny Woman's words. *Take back that which you first gave him.* Then he reared back and brought his saber down as forcefully as he could manage.

The blade sank through the gray fabric of the general's tunic, slashing through the skin and muscle of his shoulder, and shattering the bone underneath.

"No!" shrieked Jackson, but it was too late. The sword had done its damage. His left arm — the one that had birthed him like an outward womb — fell away and landed in the fire-swept grass beneath the prancing hooves of Little Sorrel.

Lee watched in horrified amazement as the thing before him began to disintegrate. Its flesh peeled away and the muscle and tendons underneath began to unravel and slip from the framework of stark, white bone. Jackson's horse fled as the fiend tumbled from the saddle and dissolved into a widening puddle of bloody refuse. Then the earth cracked open and the awful abomination that Lee had brought about once again returned to its otherworldly realm.

Shaken, Lee cast his saber aside and sat atop his horse, looking around him. Where each hellish soldier had once stood, there now lay its earthly doppelganger. The men were naked and badly blistered, their eyes wide with shock. Lee dismounted and knelt beside the one nearest him. He recognized him as the burly man with the muttonchop whiskers who had once warned him about the boy by the riverside.

"Where have you been?" he asked him.

The man shuddered, his eyes brimming with tears. "In Hell, General. In the deepest, foulest depths of Hell."

Soon, Generals Hill and Stuart, as well as Lowhorn the scout, arrived and began to attend to those who had been violently cast into the world of the living again. Exhausted, Lee turned and found the Granny Woman standing nearby.

"It is done," she told him.

"Yes," he replied with relief. Then he looked around him. "But what of Flint Wells? Did you see him?"

"No, I did not." The Granny Woman's eyes narrowed. "But rest assured, he is around somewhere. He always is."

Lee saw the severed arm of Thomas Jonathan Jackson lying in the charred
grass of the field. He walked over, picked it up, and cradled it in the crook of his arm.

"What are you going to do with that?" the old woman asked him.

"I am going to commit it to earth one last time," Lee declared. "And the secret of its burial place I shall take with me to the grave and beyond."

That sweltering summer of 1863 continued and, by the first of July, the bloodiest conflict of the War Between the States took place. The Battle of Gettysburg — named "The Harvest of Death" — claimed nearly fifty thousand casualties. The soldiers of the Army of Northern Virginia suffered gravely, unable to recover from their ordeal of several days before; an ordeal in which they had literally gone to Hell and back.

The war continued, but by the spring of 1865, the Confederacy had lost its spirit and tenacity, and chose surrender over disgrace and death. On the morning of April 9th, Robert E. Lee's final defense against the Union Army took place and, finding himself and his men, surrounded by two corps of blue-clad soldiers, agreed to surrender.

Not far from the site of the war's end, at a structure of red brick and white-washed trim in a place called Appomattox Courthouse, a single man watched from the concealment of a dense thicket. He observed not with the naked eye, but through a long, brass sniper's sight affixed to the barrel of a 45-caliber Whitworth. The British rifle, known for a killing accuracy of 1,500 yards, was held by a young man who was scarcely eighteen years of age. He smiled as he shifted his attention toward an iron gray horse and its rider. The profile of Robert E. Lee loomed in the circular lens, appearing exhausted and much older than he had two years before, but possessing he same strength of character and flawless sense of honor.

The sniper's finger gently caressed the musket's trigger. The crosshairs

settled on Lee's right temple, then dropped downward, centering on the thigh of the man's leg instead. He took a deep breath and then held it. The rifle grew stone-still and ceased to waver. His index finger applied pressure and slowly began to squeeze.

His shot was thwarted by a voice a few yards behind him.

"What is your intention, Flint Wells?" asked Granny Woman, also older, but none the less wiser. "To assassinate General Lee?"

The boy let up on the trigger. "How did you find me, old woman?"

"My assistance to the general gained me my freedom. I've spent most of it attempting to track you down. When I dreamt that the end of the war was near, I knew you would be here."

The boy's grin broadened as he turned on his heels. "To answer your question, my intention is to merely wound this fine gentleman," he told her. "A well-placed bullet shall shatter the long bone in his right leg and the surgeon's only course of action will be amputation. I will then unearth the good general's leg and use it, and all that comes from it, to march into the streets of Washington."

"I'll not let that happen," the old woman proclaimed.

Flint leaned his rifle against the trunk of a sweet gum tree and drew a long-bladed knife — an Arkansas Toothpick — from a leather sheath on his belt. "You have no say in the matter. After I gut you like a winter hog, I will have Lee's leg and do with it as I please. I have a client in Purgatory who is anxious to finish the business that you have deprived him of."

The Granny Woman did not retreat as he advanced toward her, brandishing the massive knife. "If you are anxious for the fiend's company, Flinton Wells, then so be it. I shall be more than happy to give you that privilege, right here and now." And, with that, she swung her arm in a wide arch and opened her dark fingers.

Before Flint could react, he found himself engulfed in a shower of Hell seed. He screamed as he was engulfed in blue fire and the earth cracked open beneath him. He fought, to no avail, as dark tentacles caught hold of him and dragged him downward. Within the passing of a moment, the ground had shifted back into place and healed itself.

A moment later, two Union soldiers crashed through the underbrush. They spotted the old woman standing alone in the center of the small

clearing.

"What has happened?" asked one of the men. "We heard screaming!"

"It was only the cries of the damned," she told him. "You'd best be thankful that yours weren't among them."

Then, having done what she had set out to do; she climbed atop her sway-backed mule, slapped it across the hind-quarters, and rode home.

RONALD KELLY BIOGRAPHY

Born and bred in Tennessee, Ronald Kelly has been an author of Southern-fried horror fiction for 37 years, with fifteen novels, twelve short story collections, and a Grammy-nominated audio collection to his credit. Influenced by such writers as Stephen King, Robert McCammon, Joe R. Lansdale, and Manly Wade Wellman, Kelly sets his tales of rural darkness in the hills and hollows of his native state and other locales of the American South. During his long career, he has published with Zebra Books, Berkley Books, Pocket Books, Cemetery Dance Publications, and various independent presses. His published works include *Fear, Undertaker's Moon, Blood Kin, Hell Hollow, Hindsight, The Buzzard Zone, Mister Glow-Bones & Other Halloween Tales, Season's Creepings: Tales of Holiday Horror, The Halloween Store & Other Tales of All Hallows' Eve, Irish Gothic, After the Burn,* and *The Saga of Dead-Eye* series. His collection of extreme horror tales, *The Essential Sick Stuff,* won the 2021 Splatterpunk Award for Best Collection. He lives in a backwoods hollow in Brush Creek, Tennessee with his wife and young'uns.

ABOUT THE EDITOR / PUBLISHER

Dawn Shea is an author and half of the publishing team over at D&T Publishing. She lives with her family in Mississippi. Always an avid horror lover, she has moved forward with her dreams of writing and publishing those things she loves so much.

D&T Previously published material:
    ABC's of Terror
    After the Kool-Aid is Gone

Follow her author page on Amazon for all publications she is featured in.
    Follow D&T Publishing at the following locations:
    Website
    Facebook: Page / Group
    Or email us here: dandtpublishing20@gmail.com

The Shrouded Tome: Ten Forgotten Fables by Ronald Kelly

Edited by Tasha Schiedel

Cover by Ash Ericmore

Formatting by J.Z. Foster

The Shrouded Tome: Ten Forgotten Fables

Made in the USA
Columbia, SC
31 August 2024

41367846R00100